Operation Sunflower

By

Michael Antonowicz

ISBN: 978-1-916707-44-3

Table of Contents

Dedication

This book is dedicated to the incredibly brave, suffering citizens of Ukraine, and to our God of Peace and Miracles.

About the Author

Mike Antonowicz was born and raised in the Finger Lakes region of New York State, where he graduated High School in 1974. He served five years in the US Air Force as an F-4 Radar Technician and was honorably discharged in 1980.

Following his AF service, he resided in Phoenix, Arizona, working in the electronics industry and attaining an AS in Electrical Engineering and a BA in Biblical and Cross-Cultural Studies.

In 1989, he began working in Fort Worth, Texas, on the F-16 Fighter program, and spent the next 28 years working in avionics engineering and Program Management, retiring in 2017. Mike has widely traveled and lived in Spain and Turkey for three years each. He speaks conversational Spanish and Turkish.

Mike is a pickleballer and avid sailor, though currently land-locked in Lincoln, Nebraska, with his Wife of 22 years, Renee. He has three grown children and three grandchildren.

Prologue

Beginning in October 2021 and into the spring of 2022, the world watched with fearful anticipation as Vladimir Putin massed Russian military forces on the borders of Ukraine. The buildup continued under the guise of joint military operations with Russia's puppet nation Belarus on Ukraine's northern border. On February 24, to the shock and outrage of the entire world, Putin launched a full-scale invasion of Ukraine, and American news outlets began round-the-clock coverage of the first European war since World War II.

We were glued to our TVs, watching and listening as the innocent people of Ukraine suffered the ruthless onslaught of the Russian army. We watched as billions of dollars of military and humanitarian aid flowed into Ukraine from all over the world. The supplies seemed to flow at a snail's pace through Poland and other bordering nations, even as millions of helpless refugees fled Ukraine.

Were we doing enough? How long could the Ukrainian army hold out? How could this modern-day David defeat the monster, Goliath? Could the Russians be stopped without triggering global warfare? Were there secret plans to tip the scales, perhaps?

The images of the suffering and destruction were the

backdrop for analysts and reporters and retired generals to speculate and guess . . . *ad infinitum.* The gruesome spectacle made me heartsick, and I began to wish for some military miracle that could drive the Russians out and end this horrible, needless war. In April, amid the flood of reporting, I learned of the Switchblade Suicide Drones, and I began to imagine that military miracle and then to write it. The following takes place from April 14 to April 25, 2022, code-named: Operation Sunflower.

Chapter 1: The Hut

Former Gunnery Sergeant Jerry Grazinski was winding down after a long day of sailing and working in his shop. His trademark Tony Lama boots had been kicked off and were lying beside the large overstuffed chair that he was lounging in. The flickering glow and soothing warmth of the fireplace seemed to be the perfect tonic for his tired frame—all six feet, 200 pounds of it. of it. He eyed the fire as he crushed the empty beer can in his hand, adding it to the small pile of "dead soldiers" on the floor beside him. He tossed another small log on the fire and nudged the hassock a little closer to the warmth. He was feeling pretty darn good as the softly crackling fire and the moonlight reflecting on Keuka Lake lulled him to sleep,

He dreamed, again, as he so often did, that he was in that awful hut in the Afghan mountains eighty kilometers—or "klicks"—from Kabul, fighting for his life. Then as now, there was a small fire nearby on that night a year and a half ago. In his dream, he looked up and slowly focused on the smiling face hovering above him. It was Tariq, of course, his Afghani translator and faithful friend. Tariq's piercing blue eyes seemed so close, so real. In his dream, Jerry heard Tariq say, "Hey man, it's just a graze. It's all good, man. Take a little nap, and we can get out of here, okay?"

As he slept in the comfort of his living room, Jerry

dreamed a doorbell was ringing, or a church bell, maybe a taxi honking. Then it seemed he heard a cell phone ringing, faintly at first. As the ringing grew louder, he heard Tariq's voice: "Better get that, buddy."

His eyes fluttered open as he was asking Tariq, "Get what? What do you mean?" He glanced around the now darkened room, the fire had burned down to coals while he slept, and realized his ringing cell phone had invaded his dream. He squinted at the phone display and knitted his brows at the unrecognized international number. Noting the +48 country code, Jerry shrugged his shoulders and hit the green "talk" button out of curiosity. "Hello?" After a short delay, he was surprised to hear the familiar voice of his old commanding officer, Colonel Mark Stapleton.

"Hello, I'm trying to reach Gunny Sergeant. Jerry Grazinski."

Jerry laughed out loud at that. "Yes, sir," he replied, "but we both know it's just Jerry now."

"Well, okay, I guess that's true enough, 'Just Jerry.' I'm glad I found you. If you have a minute, I'd like to discuss a little job for you, Gunny."

Jerry had not seen the colonel since the day he woke up in Landstuhl Regional Medical Center, just outside Ramstein Air Base, Germany, in September 2020. Since then, the two had stayed in touch by phone and encrypted text messages, keeping their discussions as private as possible. The colonel had followed Jerry's progress, and Jerry was pleased to hear from his former CO but not surprised. The two men had a long history together.

Jerry had enormous respect for the colonel, having served under his command on many occasions, including three tours in Iraq, two in Afghanistan, Kosovo, Syria, and many other small-force special operations. Mark was seven years older than Jerry and now a highly-decorated 26-year Marine Corps veteran, still on active duty. Towards the end of the short conversation, Colonel Stapleton added, "Oh yeah, happy birthday, Gunny. Is it today? I remember it's April-something."

"Thank you sir, it was last week on the 7th."

For a full minute after hanging up, Jerry just stood staring at the phone, considering the gravity of the conversation. Since his discharge a year ago, he sometimes wondered if he would ever see combat again. Despite his injuries, Jerry felt he was physically and mentally prepared for it, and his former commander made it clear that now he was needed for a critical mission in Europe. Jerry had often fought against Soviet equipment and Russian advisors, but this time it would be different. This time he would be dealing with front-line Russian forces in Ukraine.

He glanced at his watch. It was just after 2200 hours, and he had a lot to do if he was going to be on time for his ride to the Rochester airport in less than twelve hours.

He started to get up from the chair and winced in pain as he did. He leaned forward and gingerly massaged his right leg for a few moments. Countess operations and steel parts had made it useful again, but it would never be completely straight or pain-free, he knew.

Jerry took a long drink from the last can of Genesee Cream Ale and settled back in his chair with a deep sigh. He stared once again at the lights twinkling across the lake about a mile away. The lake was glassy still on this calm night, and the line of lights along the opposite shore was clearly reflected on its surface.

It was so beautiful here, he thought. So peaceful and comfortable, and yet so much the complete opposite of his long action-filled career as a U.S. Marine. He loved everything about his new life on this crooked lake in upstate New York, and yet he couldn't shake the feeling that he didn't belong here, that he didn't deserve such happiness. His dreams often haunted him, especially the recurring dream of that fateful day in Afghanistan eighteen months ago, the day that had ended his 21-year career in the Marines, the day that very nearly ended his life.

When Jerry first arrived in-country nearly two years before that awful day, he had been introduced to a young Afghani soldier, Tariq, who would become his interpreter, faithful advisor, friend, and, ultimately, savior. The two soldiers were inseparable and fought literally side by side in the Bradley Fighting Vehicle that Sgt. Grazinski commanded. Tariq spoke excellent English and usually sat next to Jerry in the gunner's seat of the cramped turret.

The day had started out as routine—don't they all? Jerry was nearing the end of his second tour in Afghanistan, so this routine mission was likely to be one of his last before rotation stateside. He was leading a small resupply convoy consisting of three cargo trucks and two BFVs to a forward operating post about a hundred klicks east of Kabul in the mountains. The three six-wheeled armored trucks were bracketed by the two fighting vehicles, and the small convoy moved steadily and cautiously along the rough mountain road.

There were no routine missions in Afghanistan, in reality. All seventeen men in the small convoy were on high alert for a possible ambush. The BFVs had their broadband jammers operating at full power to, theoretically at least, prevent the remote electronic detonation of any possible roadside Improvised Explosive Devices (IEDs). The road was pretty rutted up, but they managed to maintain about twenty kilometers per hour.

It was 1735 hrs local time on September 17, 2020, when all hell broke loose. The area ISIS fighters had gotten wise to the coalition jammers and, on this day, had used a more direct approach. They had buried two 152 mm high-explosive artillery shells in the middle of the narrow track.

The detonator buried with the shells was attached to a thin wire that ran up into the rocks. The deadly shells would be ignited as the small convoy wound through the rocky outcroppings. The Bradley was buttoned up tight, with Tariq sitting in the gunner's seat and Lance Corporal Steve Martinez up front in the driver's compartment. All three men carefully scanned the road ahead and the uphill slope to their right.

Suddenly Jerry felt a rush of adrenaline, and the hairs on his bare arms and neck stood up. His heart pounded as he shouted into the intercom, "Halt! Something's not right here!" The Bradley Infantry Fighting Vehicle can carry up to eight soldiers, but on that day, each Bradley in the convoy had four infantrymen in the rear in addition to the three-man crew. The four marines in the troop compartment, behind and below Jerry, opened the gun ports on the sides of the Bradley and prepared for action.

As Tariq started to traverse the turret up the slope to the right, Jerry got a glimpse of the hastily buried black wire running up the hillside from a spot just in front of their vehicle. He immediately ordered the driver to back up, but it was too late. The hidden ISIS fighters flipped the switch on their little surprise package.

The huge blast instantly enveloped the front of the BFV in an ear-splitting explosion that lifted the 27-ton tank at least a foot in the air, killing the driver instantly and mangling Tariq's left foot. Tariq continued in agonizing pain to rotate the still functioning turret, unleashing a hellish barrage of fire from the 25 mm Bushmaster gun and the co-axial M240. The noise should have been deafening inside the vehicle, but Jerry's ears were still ringing from the IED blast. As the turret began to fill with acrid smoke, Jerry popped open the commander's hatch just as three RPGs struck the right side of the vehicle, including one on the turret. That's when the lights went out for Jerry.

He would learn later that the ambush had destroyed his Bradley and all three supply trucks. The tail Bradley had been damaged but managed to back out of the trap and take up a defensive position just a hundred yards from the last burning truck. The blast had killed two of the marine scouts in the lead BFV, but the two remaining exited the rear and began laying down suppression fire. One of them had frantically set up an MK-19 40 mm grenade launcher on a tripod and began spraying the slope with deadly grenades.

In just over a minute, the two marines had killed or wounded many of the twenty or so ISIS fighters on the slope. That gave Tariq just enough time to haul his unconscious friend from the commander's seat and out onto the protected side of the Bradley. Despite his badly mangled foot, Tariq immediately began to drag Jerry to the rear of the convoy. In agony, Tariq moved as quickly as possible towards the second BFV.

The burning trucks to his left formed a partial screen, but Tariq collapsed when he was hit in the left thigh by an AK round. An infantryman who had survived from the last cargo truck scrambled over to help. The two stumbled forward, dragging Jerry through the gauntlet of AK-47 fire and RPGs. The story almost ended there, as the nervous gunner of the second Bradley sent a burst of 7.62 towards them before recognizing the men.

By the time the three men reached the safety of the other BFV, the marine scouts had fetched another box of belt ammo for the MK-19 and had resumed fire. Suddenly a pair of smoke trails erupted from the rocks. Two RPGs fired from close range had found their marks, killing the marines instantly. As soon as all survivors were inside the remaining Bradley, it spun around and lumbered back down the road as AK-47 rounds bounced off the vehicle. The Bushmaster 25 mm auto-cannon and the co-axial M240 sprayed the hillside behind them, effectively covering their retreat. It seemed like an eternity, but in less than a minute, the damaged vehicle clanked out of range, leaving a thick trail of fuel and oil.

About five klicks down the road, with the screaming of the dying drive-train getting louder and more ominous, a small abandoned building complex came into view just off the road on the left. The commander ordered the sputtering BFV off the road, parking behind a ruined mud and brick barn. They then evacuated the vehicle while the commander got back on the radio. He reported his position and situation to HQ, pleading in desperation for air support and evacuation, but as darkness fell, a storm front was also closing in. The lieutenant was told that the howling mountain storms would keep the evac choppers grounded until daylight. They would need to hold out.

The engine on the BFV would not restart, and with battery power limited, the commander decided to forgo using the Bushmaster to conserve power for the communications equipment. There were seven men crammed into the belly of the BFV: the four marine scouts assigned to it, the one surviving truck driver, and Tariq, holding the unconscious gunny sergeant. The men had done their best to stop the bleeding on both Tariq and Jerry as the vehicle escaped, but it didn't look good for either man, especially Jerry.

The lieutenant surveyed their position and decided to make their stand in the abandoned house, about twenty yards from the falling-down barn where the disabled Bradley was parked. The wounded men were moved into the hovel in a protected rear corner where the remnants of the roof offered some protection. The marines hoped the enemy fighters would not have the numbers or desire to pursue them, but they knew hope alone could not save them. They would be prepared for a fight.

Night came quickly in the mountains, and the gusting

wind brought the promise of a strong storm. Every usable piece of gear, weapon, and ration was removed from the vehicle to the makeshift outpost. They even removed the M-240 machine gun from the turret and a thousand rounds of 7.62 ammo. The weapon didn't have a mount once removed, but a burly young corporal rigged a bi-pod with a couple of branches and duct tape. As darkness fell, the Marines booby-trapped the disabled BFV with hand grenades and retreated to the hovel. Thirty minutes later, they all surveyed their stockpile:

- Twenty Meals Ready to Eat (MRE)s

- Twelve quarts of water

- Seven M-4 rifles with about 1,500 rounds of NATO .556

- One MK-19 automatic grenade launcher with one box of 40 mm ammo

- One medical kit, already partially exhausted

- Two 9 mm sidearms and a dozen clips of ammo

- One M-240 with a thousand rounds of 7.62

- Twelve fragmentation grenades

- Two helmet-mounted AN/PVS-14 thermal goggles

Jerry knew none of this, of course, as he drifted in and out of morphine slumber. At some point, a small fire was lit in the corner, and later he would remember that the warmth of it felt good. Tariq stayed by Jerry's side through the night with a pistol at the ready. At one point, Jerry's eyes fluttered open, looking up at Tariq with fear and confusion. Tariq gave his friend a drink of water and said, "It's just a graze, man. Just take a little nap, and we will be out of here in no time."

The next thing Jerry remembered was the blinding sunshine as he was loaded onto a CH-53 "Jolly Green Giant" helicopter. By then, Jerry was hanging on by a thread, heavily sedated and completely unaware of his surroundings. He didn't remember the ride to Bagram AB, the three hours in triage, or the transfer and long flight to Germany.

Three days later, he woke up in a brightly-lit hospital room. It took a few seconds to process his situation as he squeezed the call button. A smiling nurse quickly arrived at his bedside. "Good morning Sergeant Grazinski. It's wonderful to see you are awake!"

Jerry pulled the cannula from his nose and croaked a single word through his parched lips, "Water."

She left the room, returning a minute later with a Styrofoam cup and a bendy straw. Jerry gulped down the water while the nurse gently replaced the cannula. "Let's just leave that for now, Sergeant."

Jerry finished the water, took a few deep, satisfying breaths, and inquired with a raspy voice, "Where am I, and how long have I been out?"

"You are in the ICU at Landstuhl Regional Medical Center, Ramstein, Germany. You were medevaced here on Friday, September 18, from Afghanistan, and today is Monday, September 21. Please let me refill your water and get the doctor. He will be excited to hear you're awake and can discuss your injuries."

She returned with more water and turned to leave when Jerry grabbed her arm and blurted out a final question, "Wait! Where is Tariq?" She could see the desperation in his eyes and feel it as well in his vice-like grip.

"I'm sorry, but I don't know who that is. Please let go of my arm so that I can get the doctor."

Thus began the first day of the hardest, most frustrating six months of Jerry Grazinski's life.

That afternoon, Jerry was wide awake when a tall figure in Marine Battle Dress Uniform (BDUs) walked through the door. Jerry's eyes lit up when he recognized his CO, Colonel Mark Stapleton. Before Jerry could say a word, Mark handed him a satellite phone and said, "Here, somebody wants to talk to you."

Jerry couldn't believe his ears when he heard his friend Tariq joking to him, "Hey Gold Brick when you gonna quit chasing those pretty nurses and get back to work?"

"Tariq? Is it really you?" Jerry exclaimed. "I didn't know if you were alive or dead, brother!"

Tariq had lost his left foot and two fingers on his left hand. The shrapnel had been removed, but he would have a dozen or more scars. He told his old friend, "Hey, I'm fine. They gonna give me a protestant foot, man. I'm gonna try out for the Special Olympics."

Jerry chuckled at the word protestant. "Yeah, no. The word is *prosthetic*, not protestant, you knucklehead." After a few minutes, a tearful Jerry handed the sat phone back to the colonel and said, "Thank you, Sir."

Mark replied as he headed out the door, "If you wanna thank me, brush your darn teeth and shave. Some brass is gonna be here in the morning with some medals and handshakes."

So, Jerry learned Tariq would get a desk job at Bagram, assigned to community relations. His combat days were over for now, but he kept his job with the Marines. As far as his own situation, Jerry soon learned that the ambush had left him severely injured, including a ruined ear, damaged right eye, fractured skull, and a mangled right leg.

Jerry would spend many long months in Germany, undergoing countless operations and hour upon hour of painful physical therapy. His hearing had improved well enough over time and multiple operations. The skin transplant on his skull healed as neatly as possible over the titanium plate, and a very life-like "protestant" ear was fitted to his head. Several operations were performed to save his leg and right eye, though he would require prescription eyeglasses. The doctors finally declared him "healed," and in early April 2021, Jerry hopped a flight "across the pond" to receive a medical discharge from the Marines.

Since his discharge, Jerry had been busy re-entering civilian life here in upstate NY. The doctors at the VA hospital in nearby Bath diagnosed him with mild PTSD, prescribing anti-anxiety and sleeping drugs which Jerry threw away after a week due to unpleasant side effects. Jerry hated the way the drugs made him feel and decided that a busy, productive day capped off with a few cold brews was all the medicine he needed. Most nights, he slept like a brick, but that was not to be the case tonight.

The unexpected call from his former CO had Jerry's mind spinning now, and he shook his head as if to clear the fog and sat up. He decided to get an Uber to the Rochester airport rather than deal with 64 questions from his sister. Even though Janet lived two lakes east in Ithaca, she would insist on driving him to Rochester with way too many questions that Jerry didn't want to answer.

He hastily policed up the empty beer cans and put on a pot of coffee before heading to his bedroom to pack his bag for what? How long? The only thing his former commander told him was that the planned operation was "very high risk, very time sensitive, and critical to the survival of Ukraine." The earliest Jerry could get an Uber would be 0800, putting him at the airport around 0930, a half-hour late for the planned 0900 departure, but he had a feeling they weren't going to leave without him.

He pushed the questions to the back of his mind for now while he packed and prepared to leave. 0745 found Jerry sipping black coffee and watching out the kitchen window while his Uber app tracked his ride's approach. He wondered to himself if he would ever see his home again on this beautiful lake that he had come to love.

Chapter 2: The Lake

The extent of Jerry's injuries meant his career in the Marines had come to an end. When the doctors in Germany finally released him, he caught a flight on a C-17 to Dover Air Base in Delaware, where he received an honorable discharge, a gray ID card, and a fifty percent disability. It only took a couple of hours to out-process, after which he was set free with a stack of paperwork, including his DD-214. The young Marine corporal who handled his out-processing had reminded him several times of the importance of safeguarding the document. As he studied the DD-214, Jerry was amused to note that his birth date, enlistment date, and discharge date were all the same, separated by nineteen and twenty-one years, respectively. He chuckled and thought, "Okay, easy to remember those dates when I'm filling out paperwork."

His sister was expecting him at her home in Ithaca, New York, at the base of Cayuga Lake. Janet, along with her husband Dan and their two boys, had moved from Rochester, New York, about four years ago, and Jerry had never been to their new home. He was mulling over possible transportation options as he hiked the half mile to the front gate when his cell phone rang. He was glad to see it was his sister calling. "Hey Jan, I'm now officially a civilian. Hope you can put up with me for a few days. Look, I'm not sure exactly how to get up there. Should I take a bus?"

Just then, he heard the honking of a horn outside the gate in the visitor parking. Jan yelled out her window, "How about we take my car, silly?" Jerry gladly jogged the hundred or so feet through the front gate to his sister's car. They both hung up as she got out, greeting her little brother with a bone-crushing hug.

"Wow, I didn't think you would come to meet me. Must have taken all day to drive down here."

"Less than five hours, bro," as she popped the rear lid on the Subaru Outback so Jerry could deposit his scant belongings. "You look GREAT, Jerry!" I love the glasses. Makes you look very professorial."

"Well, I don't know about that, Jan, but I *DO* feel good. For a while, I was afraid I might lose my leg, but the doctors in Germany kept me in one piece at least." She pushed the button on the hatch, which cycled the lid closed, and hugged her brother again for good measure.

"Seriously, Jerry. It is GREAT to see you, and you look strong and healthy. Happy Birthday, bro! Hop in. Dan and the boys are dying to see you."

When they settled in the car, Jerry said, "I see you still are hooked on these Subarus."

"What's not to love, bro? Roomy, good on gas, and one of the safest cars sold in America. The all-wheel drive comes in very handy on the hills and in the snow, and we have plenty of both in upstate New York."

She glanced at his feet. "And I see you are still hooked on those Tony Lama boots. Some things never change."

They stopped for Arby's and a fill-up on the way. Janet explained how they came to move to Ithaca from Rochester. Dan was offered a full-time, tenured position at Cornell University. It seemed like a chance in a lifetime, so they took the plunge. They sold the house in Rochester easily and bought a large but older place close to the city center in Ithaca. Jan soon took a job with a realtor in town and had parlayed her charm and hard work into the top salesperson for the last two years.

Jerry asked how the boys were adjusting to the move. She told him that Benjamin, aged twelve, and ten-year-old Matthew were doing great in school, and she filled him in on their soccer and baseball activities.

"Of course, they have an X-box, like all kids nowadays, but we make sure they don't spend too much time with that. They are really good boys, Jerry. They can't wait to see you." When she got around to asking about his injuries, Jerry tried to blow it off, "It's just a graze or two."

"It seems to me you have had a lot of 'just grazes' over the past 21 years, bro."

"Well, I have been pretty lucky. That's how I got the

nickname 'Graze,' thanks to Tariq." After considerable prodding, Jerry agreed to relate the details of the ambush and the full extent of his injuries. She interrupted with dozens of questions, and about ninety minutes later, Jerry concluded, "Okay, you know the rest—six months of rehab in Germany, Purple Heart to pin on my chest, and an honorable discharge."

It was about 1800 hrs when they pulled up the steep hill to the driveway of his sister's home. Jerry said, "Okay, I get why the Subaru now." Dan was out with their two boys at soccer practice, so they dropped the luggage in the spare downstairs bedroom and settled on the back porch with a pair of cold Genesee Cream Ale beers. Jerry took a long pull on the familiar brew and sighed, "I have missed these. Nothing says home like a cold Genny."

The Genesee Brewing Company, located on the Genesee River in Rochester, New York, is one of the oldest continuously operating breweries in the country, dating back to 1878. Their father had a fondness for the brand and always had a six-pack of Cream Ale, in its distinctive green can, on hand. The company began brewing the award-winning Cream Ale in 1960, described as a beer that is "smooth like a lager and crisp like an ale." His sister often would send a sixer of "Genny Cream" to Jerry on his birthday, and TODAY was his birthday!

Dan and the boys soon returned home, and the group set

out for dinner at the Boatside Grill on Cayuga Lake. The boys were excited to see their mysterious Uncle Jerry, inundating him with questions. When they finished their meal, the youngest brother, Matthew, asked, "Why does your ear look funny, Uncle Jerry?" His parents were mortified at the awkward question, and Jan started to scold her son when Jerry interrupted her.

"I was hunting wolves in the mountains far away when a big mean one got the jump on me. He got my ear with his sharp claws, but don't worry, I shot him and ate delicious wolf steaks for a month."

Matthew just rolled his eyes and said, "Right. I'm ten, not 4, Uncle Jerry."

"Well, that's my story, and. . . "

"And he is sticking to it," finished Jan. "How about some desert?" Jan had ordered a cake for Jerry, and the entire restaurant joined in song as Jerry sat blushing. After blowing out the single candle, the room erupted in applause for the returning hero. Jerry was forty years old but sat ginning like a child at the wonderful surprise.

As the days passed quietly, Jerry's young nephews soon lost interest in Uncle Jerry's "boring" stories. He never talked about the bad stuff, no matter how much they prodded. Jerry himself was getting bored and began to wonder aloud to his sister what his next steps might be. They had been reminiscing about the summers they spent on Lake

Conesus, south of Rochester. She even had some old photos of their vacations there. They traded stories about fishing and sailing with their dad. Their father owned a 22-foot Catalina sailboat which he trailered down to the lake every summer.

Jerry had become quite adept at single-handing the Catalina. He delighted at pointing the craft hard into the wind and heeling the boat to its limits. The Catalina's design made the 22-foot sailboat almost impossible to capsize, but that did not stop him from trying. He lived for those days when the wind was blowing at twenty-plus knots.

As they reminisced about the good old days on the lake, Janet abruptly popped open her iPad. "Hey, let me show you something." She pulled up a web page with pictures of a quaint little 1200 square-foot cottage on a lake with a thirty-foot dock. Jerry glanced at some photos and then turned a raised eyebrow at his sister. She excitedly said, "Listen to me, little bro. This place just came on the market over on Keuka Lake and is priced right at $375k. It's on the sunny east side of the lake, just a few miles from Hammondsport."

"Are you trying to get rid of me already, sis?" Jerry joked though he was well aware it had been three weeks since he "stopped by," almost seven months since the ambush. "I can't afford that—" when his sister interrupted with a shake of her head.

"You forget, little brother, that I am the executor of your estate and have been managing your investments for the past twenty years. While you were out saving the world, I was very diligent in building your retirement fund. Remember, you saved half your pay every month for those twenty years."

She swiped through the photos pointing out the features of the home and property. The spacious living room with the beautiful fireplace and view over the lake seemed ideal to Jerry. He liked what he saw all right and paused on the picture of the dock with a well-equipped sailboat tied up. He zoomed in and whistled at the clean lines of the classic rig. "Nice boat. Does it come with? Jerry joked. Janet burst into a wide grin, nodding her head excitedly.

Jerry said, "Okay, tell me about the place."

She responded with a small stack of papers and a verbal summary. "The seller is a 78-year-old widow. Her husband died in February, and apparently, she always hated lake living and had never set foot on a sailboat or a powerboat. It also turns out that the widow has an old flame in Florida at the Villages. She owns the lake property free and clear and wants a quick sale so she can start her new life in Florida." Janet read from the contract: "All furnishings, curtains, blinds, appliances, tools, equipment, and one Catalina 27', Hull number C27870420, to remain at no additional cost."

Jerry chuckled. "I suppose you have a pen handy, oh master-sales sister. Hey, wait a minute, am I paying you a full commission?"

"Of course not!" she replied with feigned outrage. "But we will be borrowing that boat from time to time." She handed him the clipboard and a pen. "There are little arrows everywhere you need to sign or initial." So he did as he was told, and Jan took care of the rest. Thirty days later, on July 1st, Jerry signed the final papers and moved into his new home on Keuka Lake.

Other than getting a new bed and living room furniture, Jerry made do with what was in the house. He met the widow briefly at closing and thanked her for the boat. She scowled and said, "BOAT is an acronym for 'break out another thousand.' You can have it!"

The widow was right about the money. The Catalina 27 was very well kept and had been shrink-wrapped at a local marina during the winter months. It had new shrouds, lines, sheets, and sails, as well as new Harken winches. The 18 HP Yanmar diesel engine purred like a kitten, though Jerry seldom ran it except when maneuvering at the dock. The Catalina also had new plumbing, fresh bottom paint, a solar panel, and three new house batteries.

That summer, Jerry spent many days exploring every mile of the beautiful 20-mile, Y-shaped lake on *The Queen B.* That was the name painted on the transom, although Jerry was not too fond of it. Sailors are well-known for their superstitions, and it is generally considered bad luck to change the name of a boat, so he let the name remain. Jerry preferred to get out early and sail hard in the morning when the wind was up. Lunchtime would usually find him at one of the lakeside restaurants on the lake. Of course, the lake eventually froze up every winter, and he needed a winter pastime, so Jerry decided to construct a 20×25 workshop on the property.

The Finger Lakes Region of New York is full of lakes and steep hills crisscrossed by two-lane and dirt roads. On calm days, he left the sailboat docked and often took to exploring the area in his pickup. During one such road trip, Jerry had driven up and over the large hill that bounded on the east side of Keuka Lake. He was roaming along Route 226 around noon when a small restaurant caught his eye near the tiny village of Bradford. "Kozy Korner, huh?" he said to himself. "Why not?"

Most tables were in use, so he sat at the lunch counter with a few other locals. After washing down his burger and fries with a Diet Coke, he inquired of the waitress named Alice if she could recommend someone to build his planned workshop for him. Alice, who was actually the owner, pointed over to a table where three hardy-looking, albeit older men were just finishing up. She told him that the Harrian brothers were the best she knew of. Jerry thanked her and left a twenty-dollar bill on his twelve-dollar tab.

Jerry walked over to the men and introduced himself, explaining he had just moved into a cottage on Keuka and wanted to get a workshop built. The youngest of the three invited him to sit, responding with a flourish, "Absolutely." They talked a bit about the project and exchanged phone numbers. A few days later, they met at Jerry's place and worked out the details. The oldest of the three brothers turned out to be a talented draftsman and drew up plans for a pole barn structure with a concrete floor and a large overhead door. Jerry made a few changes to the design along the way, adding a tasteful-looking stone facade on the front.

The project soon started, and Jerry was impressed with the speed and care with which the men labored. They were late getting started, and Jerry had his doubts at first if they would be done before winter closed in. However, once the 6×6 poles were set and the concrete floor poured, the steel roof and siding went up in no time at all.

It only took a few days for the electrical contractor to run power to the 100-amp panel in the shop. After the lighting, outlets, and 220V industrial heater were installed, the inside was sprayed with foam insulation. The stone facade and trim went up last, and the new building was finished just as the first snowflakes began to fall in early December. On the day he wrote the final check and got the keys to his new shop, Kelly had brought along a small ice chest with a bottle of Captain Morgan and Cokes—a ritual the two periodically enjoyed thereafter.

Other than sailing in the summer and tinkering in his

shop in the winter, Jerry was a relentless crusader on behalf of Tariq. Leaving Tariq behind was his one regret, and Jerry worked tirelessly through emails, texts, and phone calls to get Tariq and his family vetted and brought to the States. Jerry believed that if any Afghani soldier deserved asylum, it must surely be Tariq. The red tape dragged on with no success, though Jerry called in every favor he could think of. He wrote letters to Congress and worked with several Veterans groups that were pursuing the same goals.

With the withdrawal of the U.S. from Afghanistan, the fall of Kabul rapidly became inevitable. Jerry's last call to Tariq was on August 8, 2021, and Kabul fell to the Taliban on August 15. Tariq said it looked really bad, and he was going to try to escape to the mountains with his family. That was nearly eight months ago now. Since Jerry had no word from his friend, he hoped and prayed Tariq had fled to safety but feared the worst.

Jerry wasn't ordinarily a praying man. He had been raised Roman Catholic, however, and found himself leaning on the remnants of faith lodged in his soul. They say, "There are no atheists in foxholes," and Jerry was no exception, having on occasion offered desperate, impromptu prayers to God above. So it was that he found himself stopping at St. Gabriel's Catholic Church in Hammondsport at odd hours to stuff the offering box and light a Novena candle for Tariq and his family.

From after-action reports provided by Mark and talking with Tariq before his disappearance, Jerry learned the bloody details of that fateful night on the mountain. The fierce firefight lasted hours in the torrential rain and wind. It had come down to hand-to-hand combat, ultimately costing the lives of three of the ten marines who went into that hut. The battle raged until dawn, when the weather broke, and the U.S. helicopters arrived. The deadly Apache gunships soon drove off the remaining ISIS fighters while the dead and wounded Marines were loaded on the CH-53 Jolly Green Giant helicopter. Of the seventeen marines in that ill-fated convoy, only seven came out alive. At least 35 ISIS fighters had been killed.

Chapter 3: Poland

It had been just eleven hours since retired Marine Gunnery Sergeant Jerry Grazinski had ended the short and somewhat mysterious late-night call from his former commanding officer, now posted in Warsaw, Poland. The call came with a request—the kind which Gunny Grazinski didn't hesitate to accept. Now here he was, on a brisk April morning, beginning his appointment with destiny.

Jerry was dressed, as usual, in jeans, a black polo shirt, Tony Lama ostrich skin boots, a North Face jacket, and his ever-present ball cap. The well-worn cap was emblazoned with an A-10 aircraft and the word WARTHOG. The venerable A-10 had saved his bacon more than once. The old tank-buster had been upgraded to the A-10C by Lockheed Martin and was every marine's best friend in the sky. A Lockheed field service rep in Kuwait had gifted him the hat, and Jerry had worn it ever since.

Standing on the tarmac at Rochester International Airport with his ubiquitous military-issued B-4 garment bag, Jerry phoned his sister advising her that he was going to 'go off the grid' for a while. "Like, what's a while?" she inquired.

"Not sure. I'm going out east for a bit."

"We live in New York, Jerry. What do you mean by out

east? Are we talking Maine?"

He hesitated before dodging further. "Further east, I guess." He was relieved to see a civilian Gulfstream taxiing towards him.

"What the hell is further east than Maine?" She paused as her question triggered stunned realization. "Wait a minute, bro. You aren't going where I think you are going, are you?"

"Yeah, no, my ride's here. I gotta go. Please keep an eye on the place, and enjoy the sailboat till I get back. Love you, Sis." The noise of the engines thankfully prevented any further conversation, so he powered down the phone and slipped it into his front jeans pocket as the cabin door fell open just twenty yards from him.

Forty-five minutes after boarding the Gulf Stream as the sole passenger, Jerry was at Joint Base Andrews, where he was quickly ushered onto a waiting C-17 Globemaster. Gunny "Graze" had spent many hours during his career on a variety of cargo aircraft, crisscrossing the world. The C-17 had more comfortable accommodations than the old C-130 Hercules, with its canvas-strap bench seats, but still, he knew it would be a long ride to Warsaw. The plane was loaded with dozens of wrapped and strapped 463-L pallets, and apart from the Air Force crew, he was the only other person on the flight. He felt out of place wearing civilian attire.

He settled into his seat as the loading ramp slowly rotated

up and closed. A young Air Force E-4 crew member checked Jerry's seat restraint and dropped a heavy parka and a couple of bottles of water next to him. Jerry thanked him and started to decline the parka when the airman said, "Excuse me, sir, but you might need it." Eyeing one of the nearby pallets, he continued, "This stuff doesn't like the heat much if you know what I mean."

The C-17 was soon air-born and leveled off over the Atlantic, so Jerry visited the comfort pallet, did the necessaries, and grabbed a snack. After returning to his seat, he pulled the parka over his lap and read a Clive Cussler paperback while listening to his iPhone playlist. After a few hours, he eventually nodded off to sleep, only to be awakened by the bounce of the landing and the scream of the reverse thrusters. The eleven-hour overnight flight had brought him to Poland at 0745 local time. Within minutes, the C-17 stopped as the engines spun down, and the port-side troop door was opened. Jerry grabbed his bag and stepped out into the Polish sunshine to be greeted by a beaming smile from his former CO, Colonel Stapleton.

"Did you get some sleep on the flight?" Mark asked.

"Yes sir, nothing but—"

"Good," said Mark. "We have a busy day." Motioning to the open rear door of the black Mercedes, "Hop in. Let's take a ride."

The ramp had already opened on the giant cargo plane,

and pallets were being rolled onto trailers as the two men drove off. Before Jerry could get out any questions, the driver stopped in front of a large hanger with dozens of workers moving trailers of equipment in and out through the open hanger doors.

As they exited the car, Mark explained that their location was Lubanik Air Base, 80 klicks southwest of Warsaw. Looking around, Jerry could see the Soviet-era air base had clearly been well-maintained and modernized by the Polish Air Force. They started towards the yawning open doors of the enormous building marked Hangar 1 in bold black letters. Pausing to let a crowded civilian bus exit the hangar, Jerry turned to Mark with a raised eyebrow. Mark replied, "That bus is taking fifty freedom fighters and a belly-full of Javelins to Lviv in western Ukraine." As the bus rolled past, Mark snapped to attention and offered a crisp salute. Jerry followed suit as those who were about to give their all rolled past them in silence.

When the bus had passed, Jerry scanned the flight line and was amazed to see a rainbow display of cargo planes using this airport. FedEx, UPS, Lufthansa, C-130s from Spain, C-27s from Italy, and C-17s from the U.S. There were literally dozens spread out in various states of taxiing, unloading, refueling, and parking. Jerry noted five aircraft in line for the main runway.

As the two men entered the hangar proper, they both

slipped off their sunglasses. The hangar was a bustle of activity, with trucks and buses being loaded. The men stepped aside to avoid a bright green 70's-era Soviet two-door Lada speeding out of the hangar. Jerry recognized the model at once from his time in Afghanistan, as most taxis in Kabul used the same vehicles. He had a keen interest in foreign cars and knew that in the 1970s, Fiat commonly sold obsolete automotive tooling to several countries, including Spain and the Soviet Union. The Lada was essentially a badly built Fiat 124, while the Spanish Seat got its start the same way. He was surprised to see one of the vintage Soviet cars still alive in 2022.

While the car was of interest to Jerry, he was equally enthralled by the driver. A pretty girl was at the wheel, conspicuous by her big white-rimmed sunglasses and flowing blonde hair. She waved and flashed a bright smile as she sped past.

"Oh man, don't tell me she has a trunk full of Stinger missiles," blurted Jerry.

That got a throaty laugh from Mark. "Relax, that's just Ailana. She's a Polish civilian attaché to the Polish Ministry of Defense. More importantly, she functions as the liaison and coordinator between arriving carriers and the 184th Logistics Squadron here on base." Jerry was all ears. "She runs a stand-up meeting every morning at 0700. She's a hoot, but don't underestimate her. She speaks six or seven languages and has a mind like a steel trap. The Energizer Bunny's got nothin' on Ailana." Jerry chuckled at the imagery. "But seriously, don't miss the morning meeting."

The two men walked down the wide center aisle of the hangar while Mark casually named off some of the stacked and stored equipment. They stopped in front of a long row of 463-L pallets, some still sealed, some opened and picked through. Mark smiled and pointed to the small green sign marking Javelin Street. "We move it out as fast as we can, but still, we opened a second hangar recently."

"Wow, that is a *lot* of Javelins!"

"Well, we call it Javelin Street, but what you see here represents nearly 7,000 of the 20 or 30 different types of man-portable anti-armor and air defense weapons used throughout NATO. The Javelins are the latest and greatest, but there are AT-4s, Tow, Spigots, Stingers—you name it, we got it. Hell, there are even about a thousand old Soviet RPGs here."

Jerry marveled at the tons of body armor, helmets, boots, and jackets. There was every weapon that he had ever heard of, and some he hadn't. The hangar floor was literally a sea of RPGs, crates of ammo, mortars, heavy machine guns, and rations.

After the eye-popping tour down the hangar, the two arrived at a door leading to a large windowless office. Mark stepped near the door and motioned toward two pallets against the office wall nearby. "Take a look at our latest play pretties, Jerry. We just received these yesterday." The cargo had been partially unwrapped, and Jerry observed dozens of olive-drab tubes nearly three feet long and five inches in diameter.

Jerry was initially puzzled—not sure he had seen anything like them before. He turned to Mark and started to ask, "Are these . . . ?"

"Roger that, Gunny. Those are the new Switchblade 300 Kamikaze drones. The other pallet is the big brother Switchblade 600 Kamikaze Tank Killer. The S300 is basically a flying 40 mm fragmentation grenade with a lot of bells and whistles. Big brother is a tank buster with a warhead similar to that of the Javelin missile."

"Yeah, I have heard about these. He turned a curious eye towards his former commander, who continued, "In case you're wondering, it's no coincidence that you and these new drones got here at the same time."

"Cool. Do I get to play with them?"

"Play? Oh, you could say that, Gunny, but let's talk about that later. Ailana just finished the morning stand-up. Let's meet the team and see what's up."

The colonel pressed his thumb on the digital door pad, and the heavy steel door opened with a click and a beep. Jerry initially regretted being dressed so casually but quickly got over it when the room panned into view. It was a big, well-lit space about 50 or 60 feet on a side. There were four doors on the right wall marked Conference, Janitor, Men, and Women. A kitchen and break area were in the left rear corner. The big room was filled with tables, desks, whiteboards, and people—*lots* of people. Very few were wearing a uniform. Obviously, these men and women were representing at least a dozen of the countries that had pledged support for the beleaguered Ukrainian people against the Russian invaders.

Mark slipped off his leather jacket, hung it on the back of a sturdy chair, then hopped right up and greeted the room with a resounding string of greetings: *"Dzień dobry, buenos dias, buon giorno, saba al hair,* and good morning."

"Boker tov," replied a young Israeli with a wave, followed by a shouted *"Dobré ráno!"* from a tall middle-aged Slovak near the back.

Mark continued, "And let's not forget why we are all here! Together now!"

His audience was obviously familiar with this morning ritual and immediately responded, *"Dobroho ranku!"* which is the Ukrainian version of good morning.

"I'm proud to introduce an old friend. He will be assigned to the land project with the rest of that team. Give a warm welcome to Jerry from America." After a bit of applause, everyone returned to their activities. Mark excused himself to confer with a couple of men who seemed anxious to complain about something. Jerry immediately sauntered over to the break area, hoping to find hot coffee and maybe a donut or two. Jerry was fighting jet lag, and the smell of fresh coffee drew him like a magnet.

He was not disappointed with the tidy kitchen. Commercial-sized coffee urns and countertops covered with pastries and snacks beckoned to him. As he queued up for a cup of Joe, he was greeted by the outstretched hand of a young, bespeckled man. "Hello, Gunny Grazinski, my name is Lech, and I'm going to get you plugged into our little group this morning, but first, let's enjoy some delicious American coffee. Please, after you, sir."

"Nice to meet you, Lech. Are you Lech, as in Lech Vawesa?"

"Absolutely," replied Lech with a smile. "My family is from Gdansk and was very active in the *Solidarność* movement in the 80s, so I am named after the great hero of Polish independence." Jerry turned and scanned the coffee mess for the expected Styrofoam cups, and before he could ask, Lech pointed out the shelves crammed with all manner of travel mugs emblazoned with logos from the likes of Lockheed, Raytheon, Lufthansa, Augusta, Turkish Aerospace Industries, and others. "As you can see," said Lech, "we have no shortage of coffee mugs from all over the globe. Take your pick, sir. You can mark your name on a mug with the Sharpie there."

"Okay, great, but please just call me Graze and drop the sir. My dad is sir, not me," Graze chuckled as he reached for a burnt orange cup marked BOEING.

Lech interrupted him and said, "I don't recommend that one. It tends to drip as the lid does not fit well." Pointing to the tall blue mug emblazoned with the Lockheed Star, Lech told him, "The Lockheed cup is better, perhaps." As soon as his mug was full of aromatic black coffee, Lech invited Jerry to a small table nearby. There, a pair of ruggedized laptops and other items were waiting.

"All right, Graze, let's get to it, shall we?" said Lech as he pushed a laptop in front of Jerry. "This is yours for the duration of your stay here. We'll begin by registering it to you by placing either of your thumbs on the biometric pad. This will also register your print for access to all controlled spaces, such as this office and the workshops." The men paused once for coffee refills and some pastries while Lech briefed Jerry on security, base facilities, and other administrative details. About 45 minutes later, Graze had been outfitted with a lanyard ID badge simply stating GRAZE and a small backpack for his laptop and satellite phone.

Graze pulled the pack over one shoulder and stood up with an outstretched hand. "Thank you Lech, *bardzow me mewo.* "

"Lech stood up to shake hands and replied with a smile. "Nice to meet you also, Graze. I see you speak Polish?"

Graze laughed and answered, "Not much. Please, thank you, and nice to meet you are just about all I got. Any final instructions before you turn me loose?"

"Not really. Let me know if you have any questions or problems, and for security, make sure you hang on to the laptop, phone, and your thumb, of course."

Graze chuckled at that and answered, "Good advice. Excuse me now. I need some more coffee."

As he was refilling, he heard a dark-haired man with a Turkish flag lapel pin mutter, *"Hassiktir!"* The man tossed a Boeing mug in a nearby trash can as he dabbed at a stain on his shirt. Well, Lech got that call right, Graze thought to himself. Just then, Graze faintly overheard the Boeing Predator representative a few feet away quip, "Big deal, Lockheed can make a good coffee cup, jets not so much. Ha!" Graze chuckled. Oh, he was going to love this place; he was instantly sure.

After Graze refilled his cup, Colonel Stapleton approached him. "Well, Lech says you are good to go for now, so grab your laptop and let's go talk." Approaching the conference room door, Jerry noted five large analog clocks on the wall. A small placard under each clock signaled local times in New York, London, Warsaw, Kiev, and Moscow. A single clock hung above these five labeled Zulu. It was 0929 local. He had been on the ground for less than two hours.

Approaching the door labeled "CONFERENCE," Mark started to extend his right hand to the print sensor and thought better of it. Turning to Graze, he said, "Let's see if Lech has you in the system yet." Jerry pressed his thumb, and immediately the LED turned green, and a click was heard from the door. Mark waved his hand dramatically, saying, *"Entrez s'il vous plait."*

They entered a conference room with four desks and chairs on the right side and a six-foot partial partition between the desk area and the left half of the room. On the other side were a dozen chairs and a ten-foot-long conference table with five or six people gathered around it, pouring over large sheets of schematics and drawings. One man was seated at a desk directly in front of them and rose to greet the two men with a big smile.

"General Smirnov," Mark said, "allow me to introduce my trusted friend Graze Grazinski. You and he will be working together." The general was dressed in khaki trousers and a Hawaiian shirt, unbuttoned just enough to give notice of his broad, hairy chest. He stood about six feet and appeared to be two hundred pounds of pure muscle. A pearl-gripped Colt 45 was holstered on his right hip.

The general took Graze's hand in a bone-cracking handshake and said, "Please, just call me Pete. I got nickname Pistol Pete during my career in Ukrainian Army for some reason," glancing down towards his pistol, with a wry smile. Pete spoke excellent English, though his Eastern European origins were apparent, notably by the occasional absence of articles such as 'a' and 'the'.

The general inquired, "Grazinski is Polish name?"

"Polish and Ukrainian actually, but I'm a third-generation American."

At that, Pete's face erupted in an ear-to-ear smile. *"Bardzo me mewo, Brat!"*

Graze knew just enough Polish to understand that Pistol Pete had said, "Pleased to meet you, brother." He responded with *"Tak dzien kuya,"* adding, "That's about all the Polish I know, sir."

The general, still smiling broadly and twisting one end of his impressive mustache, replied, "Great to have you on the team, Graze."

"Let's talk in private, shall we?" suggested Mark. He indicated a metal door at the back of the room. After pressing his thumb to the biometric pad, Mark then carefully entered a cipher code on a keypad which opened the door. "There are only three people in the world that can access this room, and fewer than a dozen have ever been in it." A small locker was outside the door where all three men deposited their phones. Nothing capable of taking a picture or recording anything was ever allowed in the Cave, as he would learn to call the room.

The men entered a fairly small, maybe 150 square feet, windowless room with a table and four chairs. Hanging on the far wall was a large blue and yellow Ukrainian flag. There was also a small desk in one corner with a laptop and two monitors. Next to the desk was a sturdy floor safe with a couple of cases of bottled water stacked on top. After locking the door, Mark grabbed three waters and they all sat at the table. The only other thing on the table was a small flower pot filled with dry-erase markers and a single fake sunflower.

Chapter 4: The Cave

Mark immediately began to brief Graze on the entire situation. "As you have seen, this base in Poland is the central receiving and distribution point for most military aid being sent to Ukraine. Twenty-seven nations are shipping, or have already shipped, an estimated twenty billion dollars' worth of military equipment, most of it handled from this location in Poland. We are talking tens of thousands of anti-tank and anti-aircraft missiles, hundreds of millions of rounds of ammunition of every caliber, S-300 air defense systems, helicopters, MIGs, artillery, and on and on."

Of course, Graze was aware from news reports that military aid was being funneled to Ukraine through Poland somehow, but now he had seen it firsthand. The brief tour of Hangar 1 and his observations of arriving cargo planes revealed the sheer volume and scope of the operation. As the equipment began to accumulate, it became clear to everyone involved that training would be required for the Ukrainians to use the new weapons effectively. Hence, the mission in Poland soon evolved beyond the collection and transfer of equipment to include the training of Ukrainian forces. In fact, several hundred Ukrainian troops had been sent to select locations in Poland for that purpose.

Mark continued with a few examples of the issues that were slowing down the weapons transfers. "For instance, the

U.S. has begun the transfer of M-114 155 mm howitzers, and several dozen of the vintage cannons have already arrived in Poland. The long-range American guns utilize separate loading bagged charges and a nine-to-eleven-man crew. Forty Ukrainian artillerymen are now at a gunnery range nearby being trained as trainers to deploy with the weapons."

"That makes sense," nodded Graze. "Obviously, the unfamiliar weapons require training, but you mentioned the MIG-29s. Is that actually happening? I've heard that the Ukrainians already fly those same jets, so what's the issue with sending them in?"

"Poland is ready to deliver around thirty to forty MIG-29s. Although it has been widely reported that the U.S. is opposed to that transfer, it is really a cover story allowing the U.S. to maintain plausible deniability for the controversial delivery. So yes, the transfer will happen. The issue is that 'same jets' is a misnomer in reality."

Mark went on to explain that since 1991, when the Soviet Union dissolved, the old MIGs in both countries had undergone extensive upgrades and modifications along divergent paths. The Polish jets, for example, had been modified to be compatible with NATO standard weapons and communication systems. The Ukrainian aircraft had evolved with improvements and systems developed mainly within the Ukrainian Military Industrial complex. To make matters worse, the original Russian technical manuals had to be translated into Polish and Ukrainian. It would take several months before the Ukrainians would be able to operate and maintain the Polish MIGs.

Graze asked if he was in Poland to participate in the training operations. Mark smiled at that and responded, "Training and logistics are not exactly a part of your particular skill set. The logistics of this operation is being done under a separate effort from ours."

Graze pulled his ball cap back and scratched his head for a moment before asking, "So . . . I'm here for *what exactly?"*

Pete answered, "No, my friend, you are not here to teach or move boxes, and neither am I. You must know that the Russians are beginning the withdrawal of their troops from the vicinity of Kiev. This is clearly a victory for the Ukrainian forces, though not for long. The Russians are regrouping in the east to launch a three-pronged assault. They plan to surround and trap the entire eastern Ukrainian army—nearly 40,000 troops and equipment. We are going to make sure that does not happen. President Zelensky has ordered a secret counter-offensive to stop the Russians in their tracks and open a re-supply corridor to the army in the east. Zelensky has committed three-quarters of our military to the counter-offensive, with a tentative date of 25 April.

Graze whistled. "Wow, that is a mighty tall order. The Ukrainians will be massively outgunned, even if the donated equipment were all in country, which it obviously is not."

Mark responded, "That's where we come in. Our role is to support the Ukrainian counter-offensive by focusing on certain key technologies and weapons systems. The intent is to integrate the new equipment onto existing Ukrainian platforms and infrastructure. If we can stop the Russians from regrouping, it will buy time for training and logistics. There are engineers and experts from across the globe gathered at several locations across Poland working on three separate but overlapping projects: the Air Project, the Land Project, and the Sea Project.

"The Air Project is focused on two main areas—the Polish MIGs and the Soviet-designed S-300 Air Defense Systems. The Ukrainians have approximately ninety functioning systems at this time, having lost nearly fifty due to Russian attacks in the past month. The S-300 is one of the most widely used and effective anti-aircraft missile systems in use today. Although designed in the late 1960s, the S-300 System has undergone countless updates and improvements and is used by over forty nations."

Pete then jumped in to say, "You probably know the S-300 by the NATO code name SA-10 *Grumble*. Each system consists of mobile radar units, control centers, and launch units with four missiles each. Several Baltic states are donating around fifty additional systems, which will bring the total in Ukraine to 120-130. Air defense is a top priority to stop the Russian offensive, as well as our planned counter-offensive plans.

"All of the systems are being modified to a common, more capable configuration. The upgrades include a more powerful, jam-proof radar transmitter, high-resolution displays, and replacement of other specific components to improve reliability."

"Perhaps," Mark explained, "the most significant improvement is the integration of the StarLink Satellite Communication system. Elon Musk has placed nearly 2,000 StarLink satellites in low earth orbit and has donated 1,500 satellite terminals and equipment to the Ukrainians, with a pledge of 1,500 more. The StarLink system is a force multiplier and will allow the S-300s to share detection, tracking, and launch data. The StarLink system is being integrated into select armored systems, as well."

"Yeah, no," said Graze. "That sounds great, but will it be ready in . . . what . . . two weeks? There doesn't seem to be time to ship all the systems here, modify them, and return them to Ukraine."

"Good point and the answer is yes, most will be ready by April 25. The S-300 team has been working around the clock, led by Lockheed Martin Field Services Division. The engineering is complete for the most part, and Lockheed is now working with Ukrainian engineers and technicians to develop modification kits and instructions for Ukrainian field teams to perform the mods in country. The systems coming from outside Ukraine will be modified here, but as soon as tomorrow, the first mod teams will deploy to Ukraine. They will be taking the parts and tools to perform the work in five separate locations in western Ukraine."

The two men explained to Jerry that apart from the Air Project effort, the sea and land groups were also working on special projects to support the counter-offensive. A team from Australia, for instance, had arrived with tons of equipment at a location on the Baltic Sea. Their expertise in sea mines and new autonomous underwater kamikaze drones would figure prominently into the planned counteroffensive.

The Australian sea drones were small enough to be concealed on ordinary fishing trawlers and dropped over the side to attack vessels at ranges up to 100 km. They could be programmed prior to deployment to navigate to a specified GPS location and surface briefly enroute for target updates via SatCom. The autonomous drones used a new proprietary sonar scrambling system, making the weapons virtually undetectable by Russian sonar systems. The plan was to have a half dozen of the stealthy drones in Odessa by the 25th.

"The Land Project or Group, if you will," Mark continued," of which you are a part, is primarily focused on the Ukrainian infantry fighting vehicles and main battle tanks. After Ukraine attained independence in 1991, it retained over 4,000 of these vintage Soviet IFVs and tanks. Most of the eight-wheeled BTRs were sold to the UN years ago to support various peacekeeping missions."

"Oh, right." Graze broke in. "I've seen many of the white-painted 'rolling coffins' over the years, with the big letters UN on the sides."

Pete said, "Well, now you know where those . . . how do you call them . . .'rolling coffins' came from. After our independence in 1991, the decision was made to sell or moth-ball about half the remaining armored vehicles that the Soviets left behind. It seemed like the right decision at the time, but after the Russian invasion of Crimea in 2014, we began a crash course to return much of that stored equipment to active service. Even with losses in Crimea and Donbas, we still have about 800 BMP-2s and 700 T-64 tanks available for the counter-offensive. Altogether, the effort will employ nearly 1500 armored vehicles, about 40 MI-24 HIND helicopter gunships, maybe 80 attack jets, 100 Turkish Bayraktar armed drones, and up to 1,000 of the AeroVironment Kamikaze drones."

At that point, the three took a short bio break before reconvening in the Cave with fresh coffee and empty bladders, and Mark restarted the briefing. "Okay, we have covered the background info; let's discuss the details of the counteroffensive. I'll let Pete pick things up from here." Mark pulled a cord on the wall, which slid the Ukrainian flag aside like a curtain, revealing a large laminated map of Ukraine.

Source: wikipedia[1]

General Smirnov then went to the map and announced, "Welcome to Operation Sunflower." There were three angry red areas on the map depicting the concentration of Russian forces near Kharkiv, Crimea, and Donetsk in the east. "The Russians are re-arming and reinforcing their military in these three areas in preparation for their planned offensive. The front-line Ukrainian forces currently west of Donetsk are running dangerously low on everything. The main thrust of the counteroffensive is centered on establishing a stronghold in Dnipro, a major city in the east, still under Ukrainian control. From Dnipro, Ukrainian forces will be in position to counterattack to the north, south, and east."

"Do the Ukrainians have the resources to carry this out?"

---

[1]https://commons.wikimedia.org/wiki/File:Map_of_Ukraine_with_Citi es.png

51

Graze asked.

"What do you mean by resources?"

"I mean, isn't that all wide-open country out there? Given the Russian air defenses and overwhelming firepower, there is no way Ukraine can win a toe-to-toe slugfest with the Russian armor."

Pete nodded his head solemnly. "You are right, Graze. The area east of Dnipro is literally thousands of kilometers of flat grain fields. A man can see five kilometers in any direction. Our old tanks and armored vehicles would ordinarily never survive contact with the Russian artillery, missiles, and modern tanks. The plan is to make the best use of integrated command and control, air defense, ambush, and guerrilla tactics to overcome the Russian advantages.

"Yes, sir, but I'm not sure how you are gonna ambush Russian armor without cover."

Pete smiled broadly and answered, "Excellent question, Graze. "How and when, and where should we ambush the Russians?

The first day of Sunflower will also include a very special mission, labeled on the map as DAGGER."

At that, Graze walked up to the map and studied the area that Pete had referenced.

After a few moments, Graze began to shake his head slowly. "Yeah, no. This looks like a black operation deep behind Russian lines. That is gonna take some big *cojones* and a very sharp dagger." He turned to look at the other two men with an expression of sudden realization. "Wait, are you telling me . . . ?"

"Roger that, Gunny," Mark answered. "You are not here for logistics, as we have said. You and Pete will be leading the mission code-named DAGGER behind enemy lines on day one. That one specific mission is the key to the success of the entire Operation. Let me paint the big picture and the role that 'Dagger' will play."

Mark explained the strategy of the counteroffensive while referring to the map. The first three days of the operation would be critical to Operation Sunflower. Pointing to Kiev and the city of Dnipro, he explained the two cities were connected by the Dnieper River, running 430 km southeast from Kiev. The river was navigable and used a great deal to move material, farm equipment, and grain between the two cities. The Dnieper was actually the fourth largest river in Europe, running from its source in Belarus to the Black Sea. The river would be used to secretly move the advance elements to Dnipro just prior to the planned counteroffensive.

The city was also of strategic importance because of the large dam just to the south with a powerful hydroelectric station producing nearly half of the electric power for lower Ukraine and Crimea. The river below Dnipro also fed a large canal system providing irrigation and drinking water for much of the same area and the entire Crimean Peninsula. It was critical that Ukraine maintain control in that area.

Mark went on with the briefing. "Two days before the counteroffensive, we will begin quietly deploying a minimum of thirty air defense systems along the river, as well as along the rail lines that run from Lviv to Dnipro. At the same time, a number of barges will depart from the Kiev area carrying eight S-300 systems, eight MI-24 helicopters, and eight upgraded T-64 tanks. They will be accompanied by 1,500 infantrymen equipped with heavy machine guns, heavy mortars, Javelins, Stingers, and kamikaze drones. Finally, there will also be one very special, heavily modified BMP-2."

Graze was pacing back and forth, studying the map while listening, then abruptly stopped, turning to Mark. "Okay, so this ancient Soviet-era armored vehicle, um, I mean *heavily modified* ancient vehicle—this BMP-2—is going to be part of the counter-offensive?"

"Most definitely, Gunny. If the counter-offensive were a spear, then the Dagger mission would be the razor-sharp tip of the spear, but let me continue the timeline. The twelve barges will be towed in three groups downriver, taking approximately 45 hours to reach Dnipro. All the barges will be camouflaged to look like farm equipment, grain, and fertilizer transports. Two of the river barges will be dedicated to logistics, including food, fuel, water, tents, and cots for 1,500 men for two weeks. The S-300 defenses along the route will protect the ongoing additional movement of forces and material on the river, as well as the rail lines."

Pointing to the map, Mark explained that the center of operations in Dnipro would be the civilian airport southeast of the city. The airport had been heavily damaged by the Russians over the past month and was largely deserted now. Upon arrival, the first order of business would be to offload the S-300s and the Dagger, referring to the BMP-2. The operation would coordinate with Ukrainian forces in the area with the goal of establishing command and control, air defense, and perimeter defense within twelve hours.

Pete provided a little background on the facilities in Dnipro. "The airport started life in the 1950s as a Soviet air base, and there is a fairly large network of bunkers and underground facilities that we intend to utilize as much as possible. Local reservists have already started opening these bunkers and removing water and debris that have accumulated over the past thirty years of non-use."

As his mind raced to take it all in, Graze blurted out another thought. "It seems possible to get the advance forces to Dnipro using the river, but it will take up to a week to move the additional troops and equipment. It won't take that long for the Russians to figure it out. Surely they will stop it."

Pete smiled. "We think the Russians will be busy with other problems during that week." Pointing to the map, he continued, "The Dagger will be a very large distraction to them, I promise."

Mark walked to the front then and jabbed his finger hard at the word 'Dagger' on the map. "Yes, think of it as a sucker punch to start the fight and knock the Ruskies off balance. We will get into all the details over the next few days, but the *Reader's Digest* version is this: We have rigged up a specially modified BMP-2, which we are calling—what else—The Dagger, complete with improved reactive armor, special weapons, Sat-Com, and thermal cloaking."

Graze laughed at that. "I always wanted a cloaking device. Are the Klingons part of the coalition?"

With a puzzled look, Pete asked, "Who are Klingons?"

"Never mind," Mark told him. "I'll explain it later. The bottom line is this: You, Pete, and four other team members will be first off the barge in Dnipro. While the rest of the barges are unloaded and defenses set up, you will travel approximately 230 km east to the Ukrainian front lines. We have arranged for a Ukrainian unit in Dnipro to escort you on the roughly five-hour first leg. After refueling and intel briefing from the local commander, the Dagger will covertly cross the forty-kilometer wide 'no man's land' to the Russian lines, penetrate approximately eighty km into the enemy rear area and attack three critical targets. If all goes to plan, you will knock out their central command facility, their eastern S-400 Air Defense Command and Control unit, and wreak havoc at a nearby airfield where Russian helicopters are massing—all before lunch."

Graze shook his head and said, "Is that all? Oh, and the Russians will just let us through their lines, just like that? Wait, don't tell me. We will be disguised as a Russian vehicle, with a big white Z painted on it?"

"Yep, you will appear to be part of a Russian logistics unit re-deploying from Kiev to the Donbas. Pete will do the talking if it comes to that. He speaks fluent Russian."

Pete laughed. "Graze, if it was easy, we would have asked an Air Force guy to do it. Together, we will deliver such a punch to the Russians that it will guarantee the success of Operation Sunflower!"

Mark pulled the flag back to cover the map and then opened the door. "After lunch, we will take a tour of The Garage and introduce you to your war chariot. The details of the Dagger mission will be more easily understood after show-and-tell." Glancing at his watch, he stood up. "I don't know about you guys, but I'm starving. Ordinarily, we take our meals here on the base, but I've arranged a trip to a nearby town for lunch today. It turns out that many Kurdish and Syrian refugees have settled in the area, and there are some fantastic Arabic restaurants there."

As they headed out the door, Mark nonchalantly added,

"Oh, and we will meet one of your crewmembers there as well."

Chapter 5: The Kite Runner

On the twenty-minute drive to the restaurant, the three men fell silent, and Graze watched out the window. As they passed a busy schoolyard, he noticed a group of young teens flying kites. Not the simple, cheap kites from Walmart. They were large, well-constructed, and commanded the wind to sail gracefully.

Mark caught his gaze. "The Afghani and Syrian refugee children have brought along their love of kites, and it has become a very popular sport locally. They don't have the epic kite battles that you remember from Kabul, but I'm told they do get scrappy at times."

Graze's mind began to spin backwards as he remembered those kite battles he had first read about in Khaleed Hosseini's book, *The Kite Runner*. His sister had tucked a paperback copy of it in his B-4 bag when he was preparing for his initial deployment to Afghanistan. He read it twice on the long military airlift flights to Kabul and gained a fascination with the kite-flying culture and, of course, a deep empathy for the Hazara—a distinct minority group in the region that was severely persecuted and considered to be third-class citizens.

On his first day in Afghanistan, while collecting his gear in the hangar at Bagram Air Base, Graze met his assigned translator, and it was as if the book he had read came to life in front of his eyes. Tariq stood about 5'8" with thick black tousled hair. He had relocated with his wife and two sons to Kabul in 2012 to begin working for the U.S. Military and various non-governmental organizations (NGOs). His English was very good, and his unusual piercing blue eyes and broad smile were ever-present.

Over the next two years, Graze became close friends with Tariq and his family. They spent countless hours together on missions and operations in their Bradley Infantry Fighting Vehicle. When the two got a break in the action, they would often fly kites in the large open areas within Bagram Air Base. They also kept kite-making material in their vehicle. A big part of their mission was community relations, and Tariq delighted in helping and teaching the village children to build kites. Graze would often participate with Tariq on those occasions, and the children seemed to really enjoy those events. For Graze, those days with the village children were the best part of duty with the Marines.

Graze learned that Tariq was a member of the Hazara minority in Afghanistan. He had been raised in a small mountain village southeast of Kabul. His father was an educated man, spoke English, and had a thriving restaurant business during the 1970s and 1980s. The restaurant did very well during the Russian occupation as they were fond of his baklava and shawarma. However, when the Russians left in

1989, the Taliban swept back into power, persecuting successful businessmen, particularly the "inferior" Hazara. The corrupt Taliban destroyed the family business and took all their money, so Tariq's father and mother fled to the mountains, where Tariq was born in 1993.

Tariq's family was a nominally Muslim family, at least on the surface. His father made a modest living in the village, baking pastries and teaching at the tiny school he opened. The school was little more than a shack with a few stools and a well-worn chalkboard. Attendance included all the children of the village, never more than thirteen or fourteen students.

The small school taught both boys and girls, though educating females was a serious crime under Taliban rule. Tariq was his father's star pupil and excelled at English, Pashto, and Arabic. It was his father that taught him the art of making and flying kites. As in many Afghani villages, kite flying was a popular hobby and often even competitive, especially around holidays.

Two loud honks of the horn and a short burst of Polish swearing brought Graze back to the here-and-now as Mark's driver braked and yelled at a careless pedestrian. They were entering the town of Pruszków and began to slowly wind towards the town center, with Mark giving directions from the front seat to the nervous Polish driver. Eventually, they pulled up next to a small restaurant, with the classic shawarma spit and chicken being grilled street side. The three men hopped out while the driver went to find a parking spot. Graze inhaled deeply and said, "Ah, I have missed this kind of food. Not too many Arabic restaurants on Keuka Lake."

They were greeted on the sidewalk by an olive-skinned man wearing a white apron. "Welcome, welcome, Mr. Mark! I see you bring your friends." Mark introduced the man as Hassan, the owner of Café Istanbul. Hassan shook their hands and repeated the Arabic welcome, *"A salamu alaykum!"* He ushered them inside to a four-top table near the back of the tiny dining area. Mark sat facing the entrance to keep an eye out for their expected guest.

Hassan excused himself to attend to the kitchen and summoned a young waiter who dropped off laminated, one-page menus and waters.

"A salamu alaykum, friends. I am Nazir, to be your waiter today. Please look the menu, and give me any questions, please I will be right back."

Mark thanked Nazir. "No hurry; we are waiting for one more person." Nazir nodded and rushed off to wait on another table.

Graze perused the menu, noting the front was in English while the back was in Polish. Smiling broadly, he pointed to the "combination plate" and read the entree out loud.

"Shawarma, kufta, humus, pita, rice and salad. Mmm, I see what I want. This place smells fantastic. By the way, who are we waiting for exactly? I'm starving." Mark picked up his cell phone, glanced towards the door, and looked up with a smile.

"He will be here any moment."

Graze was startled to feel two strong hands on his shoulders. "What the . . .?" Graze turned in wide-eyed disbelief. "Holy crap!!! Tariq??!!! Is it really you?" Graze jumped to his feet, knocking over the plastic chair under him, and grasped Tariq by the shoulders. "Good God in Heaven! It is you!" The two men then embraced as tears filled their eyes.

Tariq was shaking in excitement as he reached and picked up the chair. "Did you think you could get rid of me so easily? What am I, liver chopped?"

Graze laughed, "It's chopped liver, you knucklehead." As the two men sat down, Graze gave Mark a questioning look. "What the hell? Why didn't you tell me?"

Mark was grinning from ear to ear. "I was able to pull a few strings with an NGO and our friends at AfghanEvac in Kabul." AfghanEvac was very familiar to Graze. The group was formed by American veterans of Afghanistan for the purpose of locating and assisting in the evacuation of Afghans who had worked for the U.S. Military. The group had been unable to locate Tariq in the past.

Mark explained that the Taliban had recently adopted a more helpful attitude in an effort to convince Western powers to release frozen financial assets. A French doctor with *Médecins Sans Frontières* had visited the village where Tariq and his family were hiding and returned to Kabul carrying a letter addressed to 'U.S. Marines.' The doctor knew a former marine in Kabul working for AfghanEvac and delivered the letter. The same doctor took a cell phone to Tariq on his next visit to the area. Mark concluded, "After that, well . . . let's say I called in a favor or two at the State Department, and *voila.*"

Graze had a thousand questions for Tariq, and he began to rattle them off: "What about your family? How long have you been out? How is your 'protestant' leg holding up?"

Tariq laughed and said, "We all together arrived at Ramstein AB, Germany, just four days ago. My family has temporary housing on base while waiting for Visas to America, which I hope will be granted soon, *inshallah.* In the meantime, Colonel Stapleton—umm, I mean Mr. Mark here—has said he has a little job for me. I only learned this morning that you were here."

At that, Mark interrupted, "We will get to that after lunch. I'm starving."

The four enjoyed a long, talkative lunch, followed by baklava and many glasses of demlek chai. The demlek was the ubiquitous two-piece stainless steel chai kettle with hot water in the bottom pot and concentrated chai in the top unit. It was served in small tulip-shaped glasses by pouring the tea first and then adding hot water. Tariq was especially delighted. "I haven't had a good glass of chai in two weeks." The restaurant owner stopped by often to chat and attend to their food. While enjoying his fifth or sixth glass of tea, Tariq inquired of the owner in Arabic, "This is fantastic chai. Very fresh and delicious. Tell me, is this Rize brand chai from Trabzon Turkey?"

The astonished owner exclaimed, "Wow, yes, it is! You really know your tea, my friend. Tell me, was it the taste or smell?"

Continuing in Arabic, Tariq laughed. "No, I can see the red bag of Rize chai on the table in the kitchen." The two laughed out loud, as did the others, after Tariq translated the joke.

As they gathered outside, awaiting Mark's car, Pete was on his cell phone. When the driver pulled up and opened the doors, it seemed like a tight squeeze to get three in the back. Mark motioned to Pete, "Go ahead and take the front seat."

Pete hung up his phone and looked up at the men. "No, my friend, you may have the honor. My driver will be here in five minutes. I have a meeting with the Ministry of Defense (MOD) in Warsaw this afternoon. I'll see you this evening."

With that, they piled in with Mark upfront. Graze and

Tariq sat in the back, grinning like schoolboys. It was just after 1400 hrs when they got back to the hangar and into the office. Lech and Tariq headed to the break area to knock out the administrative stuff while Mark and Graze went into the Cave to talk.

They sat at the table, and Mark opened a folder marked "Personal and Confidential." Mark started, "I really appreciate you dropping everything to come over here and risk your neck, Gunny."

"Well, the surprise I got at lunch is all the thanks I need. Thank you so much, sir."

"You are very welcome. It's great to finally see Tariq and his family safe, but you are a civilian, so we need to go over a few administrative matters. The USAID office and DOD have authorized the hiring of civilian consultants to help in this effort, but not directly so as to maintain deniability. Therefore you are 'technically' an employee of a non-profit NGO named—err . . . lemme see here—*Hope for Ukraine.* You are under a six-month contract for $120,000, tax-free. If you are captured or killed, the U.S. Government will deny all knowledge of your actions. You will also be issued a $500,000 life insurance policy."

"Wow, I didn't really think about getting paid, but it makes sense now that I'm a contractor. It sounds good to me, but what about Tariq? I hope he is getting paid, too."

"I'll be meeting with Tariq separately, but between you

and me, I can tell you he gets the same deal. Tariq is a vetted, bonafide refugee with combat experience, so we managed to get things in place."

"Fantastic! He needs a grubstake for his new life in America."

At that, Mark somberly noted, "You should both know the odds are in favor of an insurance payout. It's a six-month contract on paper, but as far as I'm concerned, Operation Sunflower is your sole objective: a mission to end the war, Gunny. I doubt you will get a medal or even formal recognition."

"Well, since you put it that way, I guess I'm still in."

Mark produced several documents for Graze to sign, including a binding non-disclosure agreement. When they were finished, Mark returned the folder to the safe and locked it. The two men shook hands, and Mark opened the door to let Graze out. "Let Lech know we are done, and he will send Tariq back. Stick around the office or nose around the hangar and meet back here in an hour. We three are gonna take a little tour of the base then."

When Mark spotted Ailana at one of the desks, he said to Graze, "I have a better idea. Let's see if Ailana has time to show you your billet so you can get settled. We have a nice double for you with a private bath over in the former NCO barracks. I'm in the same building as is Pete." Mark went out and spoke quietly to Ailana for a few seconds, and with a nod of her head and a big smile, she waved Graze over. He shouldered his B-4 and followed her out.

When the two got out into the hangar, she motioned towards her Lada. "Throw your stuff in the back seat if it will fit." After a bit of processing, he was able to get his bulky B-4 into the back seat. "Climb in," she said as she started the engine and quickly exited the hangar. Graze was impressed to see the pretty blonde catching second gear with a double clutch action. He asked how she learned that technique, and she laughed, "Jerry, this is a fifty-year-old Soviet Lada. The transmission synchros are long gone, so the *double clutch* is not a technique; it is a requirement."

As soon as they left the vicinity of the hangars and flight line, their surroundings became much less hectic, though there were people on foot and bikes everywhere. The car windows were down, and the fresh air felt great. Graze couldn't help but notice Ailana's wavy blonde hair, wild with the wind. She was wearing the same hippy outfit as she had on that morning. This time, up close, Graze noticed a few other interesting features. He smiled to himself and thought, "Not too shabby."

They turned down a street that had several cookie-cutter two-story buildings—instantly recognizable as barracks to the former marine. She pulled up in front of a tan block building on the left. There was a sign above the door in

English that said **DOMBROWSKY HALL**. Graze remarked that the name seemed familiar, to which Ailana replied, "It should be. He was a famous Polish officer who advised the great American General George Washington. He is also my great-great-great-great-great grandfather."

"You know," said Graze, "I think there is a Dombrowski in my family tree as well." Ailana turned off the car and pulled her sunglasses down her nose to look at Jerry.

"Then," she said with a grin, "maybe we are . . . how do you say it . . . kissing cousins?" Graze quickly opened his door and clambered out, hoping she would not see him blushing.

After he pried his bag and kit out of the tiny car, and started up the walk to the front steps, he noticed Ailana was still in the car, talking on her phone. Jerry set down his bag to wait when she poked her head out the window and said, "Room 204, big guy. Oh, and see the bikes there in the rack? Use them whenever you want. There are dozens on the base. The bikes unlock with your thumbprint."

He barely got out his thanks when she started the car and resumed talking on the phone again. As she began to pull ahead, he shouted to her about a room key. She cocked her head at him and gave him a thumbs up, then roared off in the ancient clunker. Graze thought about it for a second before realizing she meant that the room had a thumbprint lock like everything else. He double-stepped briskly to the second floor, snickering to himself, "Yeah, no. Kissing cousins . . . I wish."

Door 204 popped open with a press of his thumb, and Graze stepped into a decent-sized room with two twin beds, two small desks with chairs, lamps, and laptop docking stations. There were also two office chairs and two small wardrobes. The bathroom, like the room, like the barracks, like the entire base, was squeaky clean. He did a quick 'eeny-meeny' and tossed his bag on the right-hand bed. Maybe, he thought, there was time for a combat nap before the tour.

Jerry's phone began to ring, and Ailana was on the line, "I forgot to tell you there is a small kitchen on the ground floor with coffee, tea, snacks, and fruit—please help yourself. Ciao, Jerry!" She hung up before Graze could answer. He was still full from the huge lunch, so he opted for a short nap. Twenty-one years in the Marines had taught him to sleep in short bursts when necessary. He kicked off his boots and stretched out on his back with his feet up on the B-4 bag—the classic "navy seal nap." He set the timer on his iPhone for twelve minutes and slept like a stone, waking up just before his alarm. He hit the head, took a quick sink shower, painted his pits, and squeezed a mouthful of toothpaste in his mouth. Remembering the kitchen, Graze grabbed a bottle of water, gargled it down, and then hopped on a bike for the short ride back to the office.

Chapter 6: The Garage

Four minutes later, he found himself riding up to the Hangar 1 entrance. Mark and Tariq were waiting out front, also on bikes. As Graze neared the men, he picked up speed aiming straight for them. At the last moment, he locked the rear brake and did a tire slide, skidding to a stop a few feet from Tariq. Tariq laughed at his friend's antics. "Always the showoff, man."

The two of them followed Mark as he rode parallel to the taxiway, taking note of four cargo planes readying for takeoff. Passing the last building, Mark turned left and skirted the edge of the warehouse district towards a large hangar a half mile from the runway.

The hangar was at least eighty yards wide and a little less deep, maybe sixty yards. Several massive overhead doors could be seen, some partly open, as they glided around the corner of the building. The group pulled up to a locked entry door where quite a few bikes were scattered in disarray near the entrance. Mark thumbed open the door, and the three men entered the truly enormous, well-lit facility where two fighter jets were parked directly in front of them. The aircraft were crawling with personnel and surrounded by an array of ground support equipment. Tariq was the first to comment. "Are those MIGs?"

"*Polish* MIG-29s, I'd guess," said Graze, noting the tail markings on the nearest jet.

"Actually, one is Polish, and the other is Ukrainian," corrected Mark. "They are a part of the air group's effort to study commonality and make some upgrades. Pete can fill you in later if you like."

"They are smaller than I thought they would be—more F-16-sized than F-15," remarked Graze.

"I had the same thought when I first saw them, but let's get to what we came for now. We have a lot to go over."

Mark led them away from the jets toward the center of the building. There were two very large mobile missile launchers, each with four launch tubes pointing straight up. Several smaller trailers could also be seen near the launchers, with cabling on the floor everywhere and a crush of personnel surrounding the equipment, as with the jet aircraft.

"Let me guess," Tariq said, "Soviet Air Defense Systems—one Polish and one Ukrainian."

"Close, " answered Mark. "One system is Ukrainian but the other is Czech. Their government is in the process of delivering about thirty systems for the Ukrainians."

The men followed Mark past the launchers, carefully stepping over and around the mess of cables and equipment. As they did, three tanks came into view in the rear corner of the cavernous facility. They all had seen quite a few Soviet-designed tanks over the years, and Tariq guessed T-72s.

"Nope, these are T-64s."

Graze whistled. "That is some ancient history there. I'm thinking these are from the 1970s, right?"

Mark nodded. "Probably late 70s to mid-80s vintage. Oldies for sure, but goodies."

Mark went on to explain that when the Soviet Union broke up in '91, Ukraine was one of the best-armed and most productive of the satellite states. A good deal of the Soviet military-industrial complex was actually located in Ukraine. Many of the components for the T-64 tanks and the actual tanks themselves were assembled in a plant near Kharkiv.

Mark explained further that at the time of the Soviet breakup, there were thousands of BMPs, BTR-60s, and T-64 or newer tanks in Ukraine. "During the years since 1991, the Ukrainians continually expanded and improved their industrial capacity. In fact, at the time of the Russian invasion, Ukraine was the fourth largest exporter of military equipment in the world after the United States, Russia, and India."

Tariq asked about the difference between a BMP and a BTR. Graze filled him in. "Both are armored personnel carriers with three-man crews and room in the back for infantrymen. They are both similar in design and function, with the obvious difference being that BTRs have eight wheels, whereas the BMP is a tracked machine with better armor. BMP and BTR are abbreviations for long Russian words that basically translate to tracked armored transport and wheeled armored transport, respectively."

Mark continued the history lesson. "After the Russian invasion of Crimea in 2014, the Ukrainians redoubled their efforts at modernization, even pulling some equipment out of mothballs. They completed a very extensive upgrade of their MIG-29 fighters in 2017, including advanced avionics and a radar-absorbing coating for all leading-edge surfaces. The new MIGs are quite stealthy but still no match for Russian S-400 Air Defense Systems. The Ukrainian T-64s are being taken to the next level with the best of NATO technology, armor, and munitions. The upgraded tanks will give Russian armor a run for their money.

Graze asked, "So all this work is being done here?"

"No way. Here we are doing the prototyping and testing for most of the current upgrades. As they complete each project, the teams prepare detailed instructions and kit up all the parts and components. These will be shipped to Armored Tank Plants #2 and #3 near Lviv and Kiev. The plan is to modify one out of eight BMP-2s and T-64s to this new squad command configuration. The BMPs also get some special goodies that we will see in a minute."

"Is there a Tank Plant #1?" Tariq asked.

Mark shook his head. "Plant #1 was in Kharkiv—it's

rubble now, sorry to say."

Mark glanced over at a row of locked cages on the wall nearby and motioned to a young American in khaki pants and a blue polo shirt. As the man approached, Mark said to Graze, "You remember those Kamikaze drones we saw this morning in the hangar? Sam is the on-site rep, who will be teaching you and your team everything you never wanted to know about drones."

Graze chuckled and said quietly to Mark, "A little chatty is he?"

Mark nodded to Graze and greeted Sam. "Sam, I want you to meet those 'special customers' I have been telling you about." As Mark said each man's name, they extended a hand and smiled at him. Graze noticed an embroidered logo on Sam's shirt consisting of the capital letters AV and the company name AEROVIRONMENT, all in black.

Sam said, "Great to meet you guys," and then turned to Mark. "Show and tell?"

The three followed Sam over to one of the cages, where Sam unlocked and swung open the chain link gate. Two walls of the cage were stacked with pallets and cases, and a large wooden table stood under a bright light with five or six plastic chairs scattered about. Sam started off with a short obligatory corporate spiel about the company.

The newcomers learned AeroVironment was founded in

1971 by aviation entrepreneur Dr. Paul B. MacCready, and it was a leading innovator in human-, solar-, and hydrogen-powered aircraft, in addition to unmanned drone technology. Led by MacCready, the firm built the first human-powered aircraft—the Gossamer Odyssey—and many other firsts to, including the Mars helicopter. Sam cut off his own introduction abruptly, "—and blah blah. That's who we are, but let's get to the good stuff."

He then retrieved a two-foot-long tube from a nearby shipping case and laid it on the table. "This, gentlemen, is the AeroVironment S300 Kamikaze Drone, the newest addition to our family of military drones. This one has a dummy practice warhead—perfectly safe. Check it out." Tariq reached out first and easily picked up the tube with one hand and gave Sam a quizzical look.

"You say it is a drone, but how can a tube fly? Is it rocket-powered?"

Sam laughed at that. "Oh no. The drone is inside the launch tube and has four wings and a propeller. The thin wings and tail surfaces are folded into the fuselage, as is the propeller at the rear of the drone. The wings open as soon as it is launched and spring out like . . . well, a switchblade. That's how it got its name. Here let me show you." Sam then pulled out his iPhone and opened a short video showing the Switchblade launching."

All three silently watched the 30-second video while

Sam listed the specs: "The drone and launch tube are man-portable at 5.5 pounds with a ten-kilometer range and fifteen minutes of flight time. The S300 can fly from treetops to 15,000 feet with a max speed of 160 kph. It has dual forward and side-facing electro-optical cameras and a nose-mounted infrared sensor."

When the video finished, Graze asked, "That is truly amazing, but how do you control it?"

"It is controlled with a ruggedized laptop and a small data-link device. The laptop runs our unique FalconView Sensor-to-Shooter Software, which is a common platform for our entire family of drones, including Wasp, HawkEye, Puma, Blackwing, Dragon Eye, and Raven."

Tariq passed the drone to Graze, as Sam continued, "FalconView allows import of satellite or drone imagery to identify possible targets. Once identified, the GPS location of targets is preloaded into the guidance system of the S300." Sam paused for a second to think, then gave an example. "Imagine a scenario where you have an RQ-20 Puma overhead gathering imagery. A touch on the laptop imports the real-time drone video, or stills, from the long-range recon drone.

Let's say the Puma spots a small convoy of enemy APCs eight klicks from your position. With the touch of a button, the imagery and position is transferred to an S300 drone, and it flies invisibly to a preset altitude above the enemy vehicles. As the lead APC crosses a narrow bridge, the attack is initiated, and the drone dives at top speed. The 40 mm warhead explodes on the driver's hatch, instantly disabling or destroying it. The entire convoy is halted indefinitely, and you spent just about $19,000 of taxpayer money, whereas one Javelin costs $90,000."

As he spoke, Sam grabbed a ruggedized laptop and a small twin antenna data-link device and laid them on the table. "That's it. That's the whole system." He pointed to several OD boxes of assorted sizes on the floor nearby. "If you don't want to carry these around in a backpack, we offer multi-drone storage and launch capability. It's like beer. You can buy a single can, but we all know a 12–pack's better."

"That's true," Graze said laughing, "but you still can only drink one can at a time. Can you fly all twelve at once with one laptop?"

"Absolutely. It's like a Zoom call. You can put twelve images on the screen in gallery view or toggle between individual drones. Think back to the convoy scenario. You could launch twelve S300s and attack twelve targets simultaneously."

Tariq was impressed. "Could have used this in Afghanistan, man."

Sam returned the S300 to storage and opened a much larger pelican case. He asked for help, so Mark grabbed the other end of the four-foot-long tube, lifting it onto the table.

"And here we have the big brother S600. This unit also has an inert warhead and is safe to handle as well."

Tariq grasped it with two hands and then passed it to Graze. "This unit weighs 54 pounds, and a two-man lift is recommended unless you are a Marine, of course," Sam said with a wink.

The S600 used the same common controller as the S300 but packed a lot more punch. The S600 had a fifty-kilometer range and 45 minutes of flight time. There were two optional payloads available. One was a dual-charge, anti-armor warhead designed to defeat reactive armor and kill tanks. The other warhead was a single penetration core combined with a fragmentation element effective against light armor and personnel. Either of the drones could be programmed to detonate at twenty to thirty feet above their targets, producing a thirty-foot diameter kill zone.

Mark decided that it was time to move the tour forward. Glancing at his watch, he informed the group, "Okay, that's enough for now. Let's take a look at your new ride. Sam, can you tag along?"

"Sure thing. Just give me a minute to lock up the store first." The four men then walked over to the three tracked BMPs parked nearby. They stopped at the first, and Mark explained that this was an unmodified unit, representative of the units fielded by the Ukrainians. The two rear doors were open, and the men could see a tight space large enough to hold seven infantry personnel—four on the left and three on the right.

As they walked around it, Mark described its design and features. "The driver sits in the front left of the vehicle with the 300 HP diesel engine in a separate compartment to his right." It was tracked with six road wheels per side, capable of sixty kph at best. The small electrically-driven turret on the top seated the commander and the gunner. "The main armament is the 30 mm, dual-feed 2A42 autocannon with a 7.62 mm machine gun installed coaxially with the main gun."

Mark then took them past the second BMP-2, explaining that it was the guinea pig for modifications. Coming to the third BMP, Tariq and Graze noticed it was considerably different from the stock version. Looking through the rear doors, they saw it had the same eighteen-inch wide center section running lengthwise in the compartment, which was actually a fuel tank. However, the left side was not as deep as the right. Ordinarily, there would be room for three infantry personnel, with the fourth seated near the driver and accessible through a separate top hatch. The modified APC had room for two on the left, with a new bulkhead at the front of the compartment.

Clearly, the right side of the cramped space was being used for storage. There were ten of the S600 launch tubes secured to the side of the BMP and several other pelican cases packed and stacked, practically filling the space. The lower compartment of the BMP was separate from the turret, but an intercom system allowed crew communication.

On the long rear deck of the BMP were two olive drab boxes about 3'x'3'x 4', containing 24 S300 drones. A large whip antenna was also installed on the rear deck. Two smaller antennas were on the top of the turret, as well as a mast-mounted three-foot dome housing a short-range search radar. The men then climbed on the front deck, and Mark pointed out the hatch behind the driver's compartment. "Climb in, Graze, and check out your new home away from home." Graze dropped feet-first and was surprised to land in what he could only describe as an office chair bolted down in the center and able to swivel 360 degrees.

The modified compartment was about five feet on a side and nearly that deep. Graze slowly spun in the seat and took in the features. Four flat-screen displays of diverse sizes around the inside of the compartment were easily accessible from the rotating seat. A small rack filled one corner with an array of equipment—some familiar to Graze, some not. The workspace was efficiently laid out, if not crowded. But, having spent most of his adult life inside of tanks, Graze was used to a tight fit.

"What do you think?" Mark asked.

"Well, I see it has a cup holder on the chair arm—that's a nice touch. No mini fridge?"

"Good one. This will be your mobile command post for the Dagger mission. We have added armor plating on the floor and sides of the compartment for additional protection. This machine is equipped with additional reactive armor on all sides and most of the turret. It is also equipped with a StarLink SatCom terminal, two radios, controllers for the S300 and S600 drones, and radar controls for the Honeywell AQ-200 radar."

Graze listened intently and located the various equipment items as Mark went on. "From this chair, you can access satellite imagery, launch and control the attack drones, and monitor the Radar and the RQ-11 hand-launched reconnaissance drone. Two of the small RQ-11 drones are stored in the back. The original intercom system remains as a backup; however, the entire vehicle is networked for Bluetooth communication with all crew members."

Just then, a familiar voice was heard in the hangar. "So I see you have found our new play toy. I hope you like it." Pistol Pete had returned from his meetings in Warsaw. All four men gathered on the hangar floor, and it was decided to get dinner at the base chow hall. When they exited the hangar, Pete invited them to ride in his car and leave the bikes. Five minutes later, they were parked in one of the reserved spots in front of the dining hall with a placard that said "Pistol Pete."

Graze laughed when he read the sign. "I guess they know

who you are around here, General."

As the men climbed out of the car, Pete replied, "R-H-I-P, in every military."

Tariq gave Graze a questioning look, to which he replied, "Rank has its privileges."

Inside, they found a spacious restaurant with a long buffet-style serving line offering a variety of foods and grilled items. The room was quite busy, but the serving line was short and moved fast. Graze was delighted to find Polish kielbasa and sauerkraut, as well as a tray filled with boiled pierogies. He landed a plate of kielbasa and kraut on his tray and asked one of the attendants if he spoke English.

"Yes, a little," replied the blushing young man with the white apron.

Graze pointed to the pierogis and asked, "What is inside?"

The man hesitated a bit and replied, "We having two kinds. This one is potato and this other is . . . cheese, yes, cheese and onion." Graze inquired if they could be fried. "*Tak,* of course. I will fry three of each for you?"

Graze nodded yes with a grin. He was excited to find out if the cheese pierogies were as good as his mother's. While he waited, he grabbed a bowl of steaming chicken soup and went to check out the beverage station. He found one of those new touch-screen drink machines with every kind of pop you can imagine.

He was about to select a Diet Coke when Pistol Pete sidled up next to him and said, "Are you sure? How about a beer instead?" Pete pointed over to another drink station with five beer taps and several stacks of tall glasses. In addition to Bud and Bud Light, there were three brands he didn't recognize.

Pointing to the first two of the foreign beers, Pete said, "These two are Polish beers. Tyskie Palone is a dark lager with low alcohol. The other is Zubr, a very popular, light, pilsner beer—like American Budweiser. Now the best is last, of course," tilting a tall glass under the Obolone tap. "Look at that, Graze," cooed Pete as he deeply inhaled the aroma from the filling glass. The golden lager had a soft foamy head and crisp aroma of grassy hops. Graze accepted the invitation to fill his own glass with the "pride of Kiev."

The four took seats at a table near a big window overlooking a manicured courtyard. Graze was not surprised when Tariq sat down with two fully dressed cheeseburgers and a mountain of hot stringy fries. They ate in silence for a minute or two until Tariq finished wolfing down a burger and let out a big sigh. Graze smiled at his friend. He knew Tariq would exist exclusively on burgers, fries, and Coke if given the chance. "How's the burger?"

"Oh man, it's SO good! It's been two years since I had a good burger and fries, Graze. How is the Polish food, buddy?

As good as your mom's?"

"Well, if my mother were here, I'd say 'of course not,' but in truth, it's pretty darn good."

The men made small talk during the meal, but when Graze asked a question about the Switchblade drones, Mark shushed him and whispered, "Loose lips. We'll convene in the Cave after dinner and dig into the details."

At 1815 hours, they deposited their trays on the belt and headed outside into the cool Polish evening. They agreed to walk back to Hangar 1, and Graze was happy to see the natural gait that Tariq had developed with his artificial foot. Pete lit up a Marlboro Red, and Graze took note of the battered silver Zippo lighter in his hand. "Old school," he thought. It took about fifteen minutes to reach the hangar, and Mark decided to call it quits for the day.

Chapter 7: Trap Door

Naturally, Tariq and Graze shared room 204 at Dombrowsky Hall. Climbing the stairs to the second floor, Tariq joked, "I suppose you still snore like a chainsaw."

"No, man, I once stayed up all night to listen and never heard a sound." They both laughed at the corny joke. Graze left his friend to settle in and shower while he checked out the kitchen on the ground floor. The refrigerator had several bottles of Polish beer and a donation can on the shelf that read "Beer 1 Euro." He hadn't exchanged any money yet, so he dropped two bucks in the can, grabbed an ice-cold Tyskie, and headed to the front steps.

As he relaxed and soaked in the last of the day's sunshine, he reviewed the last 24 whirlwind hours of his life. It was a lot to process, and he was bone tired and ready for some shut-eye. As he took the final swig of his beer, he was pleasantly surprised to see a lime green Lada pull up at the curb. Ailana popped her pretty head out the window and said, "Hi Jerry, I see you found the beer."

He tipped the empty bottle in her direction. "Yes, ma'am. All the comforts of home."

The door of the ancient car squeaked loudly as she climbed out with a small cooler. "Mind if I join you?" It seemed to be a rhetorical question as she sat on the step beside him before he could answer. Jerry really was exhausted, but the arrival of this fascinating woman woke him right up.

"You might as well drink a good *piwo,* not that commercial crap." She retrieved two bottles of Artezan beer and popped the tops with a bottle opener hanging from her keychain.

"Nice," thought Graze, "she comes prepared." As they drank their beers, they quietly exchanged a bit of their stories and got to know each other a little. He told her about some of the places he had been, though being careful not to mention combat or warfare. He learned that they were both single, having never married. She had been living on base for the past six weeks, although she owned an apartment in the Praga district of Warsaw—east of the Vistula river and apparently the nexus of the up-and-coming "boho" movement in Warsaw. That made sense to Graze as he pondered her frayed jeans, tie-dyed blouse, and peace-sign necklace. They chatted for nearly an hour; then she roared off in her car, which was named Oscar after Oscar the Grouch from *Sesame Street.* Tariq was already sound asleep when Graze got to the room, and ten minutes later, they were both snoring.

In the morning, Graze woke to find Tariq on his prayer rug doing morning prayers, so he showered and headed downstairs for coffee. Twenty minutes later, Tariq joined him and five or six others enjoying coffee and fat round jelly-filled pastries called *Pączki* (pronounced "pohnch-kee"). They then biked to Hangar 1 and arrived at the office just as Ailana was starting her morning briefing.

She summarized the material processed in and out during the past 24 hours and then made some important announcements. "Tomorrow, April 17th, is Easter Sunday and an official government holiday. You are all free to continue working, of course, but there will be limited services available. The Logistics branch will be closed; therefore, it is very important that all requisitions for parts or material be submitted by noon today." She repeated that last sentence in four or five languages, just to be sure. "Also," she added, "the base restaurant will NOT be open for breakfast or lunch, but several ice chests of sandwiches will be brought to this office tonight for your dining pleasure." The crowd murmured approval.

"The good news is that our fantastic kitchen staff will be coming in after church to prepare a wonderful Easter dinner with ham, duck, potatoes, and many other delicious Polish foods. Easter dinner will be served from 1630 to 1800. Now, if there are no questions . . ." Pausing for a few moments, she continued, "Then let's get to work. Please remember the noon deadline today for requisitions, or you must wait until Monday."

The room slowly emptied as Ailana mingled and

collected a few requisition forms. She caught Graze's eye and waved him to her. "I have it on good authority that you will be having the day off tomorrow as well. I'll come by the barracks tonight at 1800 with good beer and a proposition for you. Stay tuned," she added with a coy wink.

Mark, Graze, Pete, and Tariq conferred for a moment, and then Mark led the group out the back door to a waiting van. It was one of those airport shuttle vans, with the rearmost seats removed for cargo, leaving seating for ten. Sam, from AeroVironment, was already seated, along with three men that Graze did not know. The men were dressed in jeans and T-shirts, but their GI-issued boots and demeanor hinted to Graze that these were the three other members of the Dagger crew. There was also a large pile of olive drab tubes, pelican cases, and some ice chests in the cargo space. As they set off, Mark explained that their BMP had been trailered to an artillery and bombing range about thirty klicks from the base. Today would begin a week of intensive training.

Pete introduced the three Ukrainian soldiers (as Graze had guessed), and hellos and handshakes were exchanged in the crowded van. "These men are all seasoned combat soldiers that have been hand-selected by me for the Dagger mission. The criteria I used were experience and fluency in Russian and English." One of the men mumbled something to Pete in Ukrainian, and General Smirnov corrected himself. "Okay, fluency in Russian and 'pretty good'

English." Pointing to the youngest of the three, he explained that Dmytryi was 26 years old from the city of Mariupol and had spent the last seven years fighting in the Donbas and could drive anything that moved. He was an excellent mechanic as well and especially familiar with the BMP-2. "He will be our driver."

Pointing to the man next to him in the middle seat, Pete introduced Aleksandr, a 33-year-old professional soldier from Kharkiev. He had combat experience in Crimea, Donbas, and, most recently, in his hometown before the Russian takeover. "He has experience in anything that blows up, including artillery, mortars, IEDs, and landmines. He will be in the back with Pavel and is also backup driver.

"Pavel is 34 years old, from our beautiful capital city. His expertise is … killing Russians with anything he can get his hands on," he said with a grin. "Pavel is also a very good cook." None of the men had families or children, and Graze thought to himself that may have been an unspoken criteria for inclusion, given the nature of their mission.

They continued in relative silence for the remainder of the trip, with the exception of Sam – the guy *loved* to talk. As they approached the security entrance at their destination, the driver pressed his thumb on the drive-through bio-reader, which swung the gate open. The guard seated nearby looked up from playing Candy Crush long enough to wave. Once inside, they drove onto the range towards a lone BMP parked on the edge of the field, backlit by the morning sun and glistening with dew. The driver parked between the armored vehicle and a canopy covering two large picnic tables. The driver's tasks were done until lunchtime when he would be expected to retrieve the ice chests for lunch.

Mark, Sam, and Dagger crew exited the van, and Sam opened the rear doors asking for help getting the kamikaze drones onto one of the tables. There were twelve of the smaller S300s and two of the big S600s in their launch tubes. The men also removed a toolbox and two large pelican cases. Once the van was unloaded, Mark gathered the group near the armored vehicle and began the briefing.

"This is going to be your home for the next few weeks." The men inspected the fifteen-ton vehicle as Mark related its history. Manufactured in Russia in 1982, it was delivered to the Ukrainian army soon after. This particular vehicle was mothballed from 1997 to 2017. At that time, it was sent to the Lviv Armored Vehicle Factory and refurbished and upgraded to the BMP-2A configuration. The engine and drivetrain were overhauled, the suspension upgraded, and new tracks and road wheels were installed. The radios and all electronics had also been upgraded, including new sighting systems for the gunner and commander. All of the men had been briefed on the planned Dagger mission, so no one was surprised by the Russian markings.

Tariq, of course, had not been following news of the war

and asked, "Why is there big letter Z's painted on it?"

Pete was quick to respond. "Well, Tariq, soon after the invasion started, all Russian military vehicles started to display the Z, maybe to avoid confusion since both our armies have many of the same types. Why Z? No one really knows, but some Russians say it stands for *zapad,* meaning west in Russian. It has become a propaganda symbol for the war. Putin gave free Z T-shirts to all the schools, and Russian children wear them on special days." Then he added very sarcastically, "to honor the glorious liberation of Ukraine from the Nazis."

"Ukrainians believe the Z stands for *zhopa,* which is what we think about their army." The Ukrainian NCOs burst out laughing and nodding in agreement at that. Pavel blurted out, "It means ass!" Graze laughed too and thought to himself, "Makes sense. In Polish, the word is *dupa.* "

Once the laughter died out, Mark continued the briefing. "This morning, you will start training with the kamikaze drones until you can fly them down an open T-80 hatch at 40 km. Every crew member will become proficient at using the vehicle-mounted weapons as well as the drones, including the RQ-11 short-range recognizance drones. Everyone must also learn the Javelin and Stinger missile use. Mark glanced at his watch and told the crew, "I'll leave you to it now and check on you guys after lunch. I have a meeting with the brass in Warsaw in thirty minutes."

Pete said with a frown, "Warsaw is 90 kilometers from here. You are gonna be late, boss."

His warning was interrupted by the sound of an approaching helicopter that landed fifty yards from the Dagger. Mark grabbed his laptop bag and said with a smile, "I'll be there in plenty of time." He covered the ground to the helicopter at a crouching run and hopped in the open door of the sleek craft.

Sam continued the briefing, explaining that the morning would be devoted to hand-launch, flight control, target acquisition, and attack modes of the S300 and S600 drones. He pointed to a spot about five hundred yards out in the field where a pole-mounted red flag could be seen. "That flag is marking a practice target that we will be using today. You will see later that a pit has been dug, filled with inflatable air mattresses, and covered by a strong nylon net. Life-sized paper silhouettes of Russian-armored vehicles will be stretched across the netting."

Each of the men would get turns to kill paper tanks, using first the smaller S300 units and progressing to the S600s. All drones were equipped with dummy warheads installed, but they would have the same flight and maneuver characteristics as the actual armed drones. Sam informed them, "The drones you are using will behave exactly as they will in combat, with one exception—they don't blow up."

Pavel frowned. "So we don't get to actually blow up

stuff?"

"Oh yes, there are several derelict tanks and helicopters out on the range here, but first, you will learn the basics with these practice drones. You will become experienced at flying them at night and hopefully in the rain as well. Gather round, and I'll give a brief tutorial on the control tablet and the drones themselves."

Sam then launched one of the small drones and demonstrated the flight and sensor controls to the spellbound group. The men were amazed at the resolution and stability of the EO (electro-optical) and IR (infrared) sensors. From an altitude of two thousand feet, they were easily able to see details on the ground. Sam had the group smile and wave as he captured a picture that he displayed on the screen. They all laughed when Sam zoomed in on the image revealing Pavel holding up his middle finger.

The group spent the next several hours attacking the paper tanks. They also took several trips to the pit on the BMP to inspect their accuracy and recover spent drones. As lunchtime approached, the men were feeling confident and started making bets on who could hit the commander's hatch on the paper tank. Just before lunch, they recovered the last of the drones, and a grinning Tariq collected on the bet. They headed back to the picnic table where the driver had set out the ice chests with food and drink.

Sam promised to pull out the "big gun" after lunch,

meaning the 54-pound S600 tank buster. While they ate, Sam did a show-and-tell laying out its specs. The men were amazed at the precision and technology of the switchblade drones. It was very obvious to all of them that these new weapons were true game-changers on the modern battlefield. Pavel asked Sam if there were names for them, like Raven or Hawk or something clever. Sam related that the workers at Aerovironment usually called them Tweety Bird and Big Bird. Everyone recognized Big Bird from Sesame Street, and after the Ukrainians did a Google image search on Tweety Bird, the names were unanimously accepted.

Sam explained that during the mission, the Big Birds were intended to be launched from the turret of the Dagger and controlled by either the tank commander or mission commander. He pointed out the brackets that had been added to both sides of the turret, where four launch tubes could be mounted. He went on to say that the Big Birds were much heavier and would often tear through the target netting and become damaged. Since the larger drones had a long flight time, they would launch only one of the inert drones and take turns operating the flight and sensor controls. The men drew straws for the honor of conducting the simulated attack on the paper tank, which Pete won.

As soon as the excited men finished lunch, Aleksandr and Pavel launched a Big Bird from the turret of the Dagger while Dmytryi operated the control device. The next 35 minutes were spent flying above the practice range, with everyone taking turns at the controls. When the low battery light flashed on, Pistol Pete took the controls and guided the drone to the target pit from an altitude of five thousand feet. The other men scanned the skies to see the drone, but even when directly overhead at an altitude of 5,000 feet, it was virtually invisible to the naked eye. On Sam's cue, Pete locked onto the turret of the T-80 silhouette and began his attack.

The killer dove at 125 mph, taking less than thirty seconds to reach the target. During recovery of the drone afterwards, they noticed Pete had just missed the turret, scoring a direct hit on the engine compartment behind it. Pete seemed disappointed, but Sam reminded him that it was still a "kill shot" as the tank would be completely disabled at a minimum. Around 1400 hrs, as the team was discussing what they had learned, the EH-101 returned, depositing Colonel Stapleton on the ground and immediately returning to the air.

Mark reported that he had some good news from the brass that he would share later. In the meantime, the men should load into the BMP and practice maneuvers, with the men rotating between positions. There were a couple of derelict vehicles a few miles out that they would attack at various speeds and angles with the 30 mm autocannon. After the Dagger departed for gunnery practice, Mark enjoyed a sandwich and caught up on email at the picnic table. At 1600 hrs, the Dagger returned and was loaded back onto the transport vehicle. The men packed all the gear back in the van and started back to the base. Mark and Pete exchanged smiles as they listened to the excited chatter from the newly formed crew.

Arriving back at the garage around 1640, Mark released the men for the day, but before they scattered, he pulled Graze aside and told him that he would have Easter Sunday off.

"Thanks, Colonel, but I'll be glad to continue training with the crew if you want me to."

"Look, Gunny, there will be nothing for you to do. The mission vehicle will be unavailable until Monday undergoing further modifications. The rest of the crew will spend a half day getting training on the RQ-11 drones and Javelin and Stinger missile systems. We both know you are an old hand at wrangling that gear, so take the day off."

"Well, okay. I think Ailana has some plans for tomorrow. I guess I could use a day off, especially with her," he added with a shy grin.

Mark smiled at that and replied, "She certainly is an interesting person. I'm sure you will have fun, Gunny."

Quickly changing the subject, Graze asked, "What modifications are planned for the Dagger?"

Mark explained that the Finnish Army operated the same old Soviet BMPs and had developed a few new tricks for the old dog. A team of engineers had arrived and would begin work immediately on their upgrades to the Dagger, which included a bolt-on exhaust gas turbocharger that could be fitted to the Dagger.

"It will add approximately 75 horsepower to the underpowered vehicle and increase top speed to 75 kph. The Finns have also developed a proprietary thermal masking system to be added to the engine compartment for stealth." Just then, Pete's car pulled up to them, and Pete motioned from the front seat for the two men to join him. Mark motioned towards the car, saying, "Let's take a ride. There is one more thing that Pete and I would like to show you."

As they drove, Pete explained to Graze that he was absolutely correct on the risks of engaging Russian armor on the open plains, but there could be a way to even the odds. They were driving past a huge wheat field that bordered the base when Pete ordered the driver to stop near a wide gate in the fence. Leaving the car on the road, Pete thumbed them inside the field and explained that this 100-acre wheat field was typical of the fields found in Eastern Ukraine. The grain was nearly knee-high. Pete pulled out some reconnaissance photos of the field taken at various altitudes and showed them to Graze. Looking out at the field, he said, "Okay, it's a wheat field, right on."

"Is it, Graze? Is that what you see? Walk with me." The two followed Pete as he took a circuitous path out into the field. After about five minutes of walking, Pete stopped and said, "Well, do you still see a wheat field?"

Graze nodded his head slowly as if he had been asked a dumb question.

"PERFECT!" Look carefully right over there."

As Pete pointed to a spot in the field about twenty feet away, Graze could now see a small object that looked like an iPhone poking up about six inches above the wheat. Pete then yelled an order in Ukrainian, and a hand appeared next to the object and began a friendly wave. "I would like to introduce you to the 'Trapdoor Project,'" said Pete proudly. Pete and Mark then stepped a few feet further and pulled back the corner of a very sophisticated camouflage net, revealing a five-foot deep, ten-by-ten foxhole.

Squatting slightly and peering inside, Graze was surprised to see three Ukrainian soldiers smiling and waving to him. "What in the blazes am I looking at?"

Pete then explained, "You rightly stated that ambush of Russian armor would be impossible without buildings or trees to hide behind. This is not the first time, however, that the Ukrainian army has faced this challenge. During the German attack on the Soviet Union in June 1944, German tanks, supported by artillery and air power, were sweeping east through many of these same fields. A desperate plan was devised wherein solitary soldiers were hidden in shallow pits covered by crude camouflage. When German tanks passed close, the men would spring out and throw a satchel bomb into the treads of the Panzers. No one is sure exactly how effective this tactic was, as none of the ambushers lived to talk about it. So here we have improved that concept with modern technology."

He barked another command, and the three Ukrainians inside scrambled out of the trench on a small ladder. Pete then climbed down and invited Graze to follow. As it was almost dark inside, Pete reached to a small switch panel on a pelican case and an array of LED lights attached under the top covering that lit up the interior. Pete explained that the traps could be set up and staffed in less than three hours. On the night of arrival in Dnipro, while Graze and the crew departed on their mission, Operation Trap Door would also commence.

Once inside, Pete explained and pointed out the equipment and supplies. The four helicopters on the barges would deploy to set the traps within hours of arrival. They had worked out a technique using a specially designed warhead fitted to an RPG that would be fired straight into the ground from a hovering helicopter. The blast would create a crater surrounded by a ring of displaced earth.

Five small pallets of equipment and three soldiers would be quickly offloaded, and the helicopter would return to

Dnipro for the next load. Using four helicopters, they would set up a defensive half-ring of twelve ambush sites on a roughly 50-kilometer radius from Dnipro—all on the first night.

There were two large six-foot-long cases containing a total of six S600 attack drones. Pete pointed out that the cases also doubled as beds, and Graze could see there were air mattresses and sleeping bags on them. The bottom of the pit had a plywood floor, and there was a small hole in the lowest corner of the space with a sump pump in case rainwater caused problems. In the center was what looked like a double-sided step ladder with a mast on top. This held up the center of the canopy, supported communications and surveillance equipment, and allowed the soldiers to climb up and fire weapons.

Pointing to one of the other large cases, Pete said, "That holds a powerful lithium-ion battery unit and inverter to power everything. To keep the power packs charged, there is also a small 2K generator and thirty liters of fuel to run it periodically. There you see the drone control unit and a SatCom terminal. It is a completely self-contained and invisible position with food and water to last three men for two weeks. Graze noted that one light was directly above a small table, with two cups of still-steaming tea on it and some playing cards.

"All the comforts of home," agreed Graze. "The

efficiency and firepower is impressive, and the camouflage is amazing."

Thank you, Graze. The camouflage canopy is a sophisticated cover with three layers. The bottom layer has a reflective coating to keep heat from escaping. The next layer is waterproof reinforced nylon, and the top layer is produced in a carpet factory in Krakow. It is a lightweight synthetic base material with the fake wheat plants carefully glued to the top."

Pete explained the plan is for individual "Trap Door" locations to be notified when enemy targets are within the fifty-kilometer range of the Big Birds. HQ would order the attack and send GPS coordinates. There were several zippers sewn into the camouflage to allow the men to poke the S600 out and launch discreetly. "As the enemy forces move within range, we will knock them out. The deadly surprise attacks will slow them down, and they will have no way of knowing where the attacks are coming from."

Graze and Pete climbed out after about twenty minutes, and the Ukrainian soldiers returned inside. As soon as the camouflage was pulled back in place, the three men headed back towards the car. After a dozen steps, Graze stopped to look back. "Absolutely amazing, General. Pure genius! Did you say you are ready to deploy these traps around the base in Dnipro?"

"Yes. We have gathered everything to deploy all twelve

operational sites. This test position was actually set up by the three soldiers here two nights ago in six hours."

Mark added. "We are still short 20 of the S600 drones, but they are expected to be delivered in two days."

As soon as the tour was finished, the group headed straight to the chow hall, where Jerry gulped down some pierogies and then peddled as fast as he could back to the barracks. Arriving just before 1800 hrs, he threw the bike down and ran upstairs. After a thirty-second sink shower, a fresh shirt, and a dash of Christian Dior Fahrenheit, he flew down the stairs, stopping on the way to grab a beer. At 1808 hrs, he was sitting on the front steps, trying to look casual. His heart was pounding, and a bead of sweat trickled down his forehead. He thought to himself, "What the hell, Jerry? You are acting like a teenager."

After ten minutes of anguish and self-doubt, he downed the beer and started back inside, muttering to himself about being a damned fool. As his hand reached the door, he heard the beep-beep of the Lada. He turned in time to see Ailana pull up to the curb. She laughed and called out, "Don't give up yet, Jerry. I'm just running a bit late. You don't think those fools all turned in requisitions by noon, do you?"

Chapter 8: Ailana

Ailana suggested they drive to a better spot to visit. About five minutes across the base, they found a quiet playground that was largely deserted, aside from a few ducks wandering around. They sat at a low table, with the cooler of beer handy, and talked for at least an hour.

Jerry learned that Ailana had been born and raised in the city of Bialystok, in the far east of Poland. Her father was a high school teacher, and her mother a nurse at one of the hospitals in the city. She had two older brothers. The eldest, Stephan, was an F-16 aircraft technician in the Polish Air Force stationed at the 31st Tactical Air Base near Poznan.

Jerry was aware that Poland had around fifty F-16s, and he wondered what Stephan's job was. She didn't know exactly but knew it was in electronic testing—something called ASI or AIS, perhaps. He didn't recognize the acronym, but he was reminded of his father, Charlie, who had been a WCS radar technician on the venerable F-4 Phantom back in the day. Growing up, Jerry had heard many stories about Utah and Torrejon, Spain. His sister, Janet, had been born at Hill AFB, Utah.

"How far is Poznan from here? Do you see him often?"

"Sadly, no. Poznan is about four hours' drive, and he has a family with two young girls to keep him quite busy."

Her other brother was her "Irish twin," having been born just ten months before her. His name was Michal (pronounced mi'-how), and he was a caretaker and game warden for the great herds of bison in the Bialowieza Forest near Bialystok.

"Bison in Poland? I didn't know there were bison in Europe."

"Poland is home to nearly all of the European bison, with over two thousand alone in the preserve where my brother works."

"Wow, what an interesting job. So he is basically a bison rancher?"

"Farmer, yes."

"Well, in English, we would say rancher, not farmer."

"Correct, and the polish word for rancher is farmer."

"Oh . . . weird."

Ailana continued to relate that she had left home after high school graduation and attended the Jagiellonian University in Krakow, achieving degrees in cross-cultural studies and literature. He asked her if her university studies were the reason she was fluent in so many languages. "Yes and no. My hometown is sort of a melting pot of people and culture, and it is very common for people there to speak three or more languages. I did study French, Italian, and English at university, though."

After Krakow, she moved to Warsaw, where she had lived for the past eight years. Jerry did some mental calculations and guessed she must be 30 or 31, probably way too young for a beat-up forty-year-old Marine.

It didn't take Jerry long to tell his story when asked. "I was born and raised in a beautiful part of New York state, joined the U.S. Marines at age 19, served 21 years, and retired to a house on a lake in the same area." He talked of his sister and nephews in Ithaca and mentioned his love for sailing. At that, Ailana perked up. She told him she loved to watch sailboats, mostly on television, and hoped someday to actually sail on one.

He replied with a smile, "I have an eight-meter boat at my home. Maybe someday I can teach you to sail if you ever visit America."

"Inshallah, Jerry, *Inshallah."* He was surprised to hear her speak the phrase "God willing" in Arabic, but she quickly informed him that was the extent of her skills in that language.

Eventually, she got around to her promised proposition for Sunday. She wanted him to go to Warsaw with her and attend Easter Mass. She needed to visit her flat in the Praga district and run a few errands as well. She was eager to show off the beauty of Warsaw to her new friend. Jerry remarked to her that he didn't have a suit or even a sport coat with him, but she dismissed his excuse with a wave of her hand. "If you have a clean shirt and trousers, you will be fine. After church, we could also attend a special new exhibit that has just opened in Warsaw."

Jerry happily accepted the invitation and agreed to meet her at 0900 at the barracks. As they drove back across the base, Jerry wondered to himself if the old Soviet jalopy could make the ninety-minute drive and politely suggested as much to Ailana. She feigned outrage and assured him that, despite outward appearances, her Oscar the Grouch was very well-maintained. She then turned on the radio to show off the new sound system she had installed. An FM station was playing classic rock, so he asked her to turn it up. By the time they reached the barracks, they were both singing the final verses of "Hotel California." They said goodnight, and he skipped up the stairs to his room.

As he thumbed his way into room 204, he was happy to see Tariq's shoes in the hallway with a can of Lysol next to them. He loved his friend Tariq with all his heart, but man, he had some smelly darn feet. Well, at least one was still a stinker, he thought with a chuckle. He gave the shoes a shot of Lysol for good measure and went inside. Tariq was already sleeping, and Graze decided to head for bed as well. He would shower and shave in the morning. After 21 years in the marines, his internal clock woke him at 0530 without fail, but he set the alarm on his iPhone just to be sure. He slept like a log, awakening a few seconds before his alarm.

Tariq was still sleeping, but Graze knew he would be up soon on his special prayer rug doing the *ṣalāt al-fajr,* or morning prayer, as he did every morning. Graze was accustomed to this Muslim practice and typically gave his friend privacy when it was possible. He threw on a pair of sweatpants and a Pink Floyd T-shirt and headed down to the mess for coffee and, hopefully, something to eat. As he was leaving, he gave Tariq's bed two solid bumps. Tariq stirred a little, and Graze said, *"Saba al hair.* I'm going downstairs for coffee, so—"

"Yeah, yeah, I know . . . good time for my magic carpet ride."

"Mashallah," Graze answered as he grabbed his trusty Lockheed mug and slipped out the door.

One or two people were in and around the mess. There were two of those large stainless steel coffee urns—one ready and one still percolating. Graze filled his mug and inspected the refrigerator. He found containers with sliced tomatoes, sliced white cheese, and some kind of sliced salami-looking meat and mayonnaise. Glancing over at the loaves of bread on the counter, he thought to himself, "Okay, breakfast sandwich it is."

He sat down at one of the small tables with a hastily folded *USA Today* on it. The newspaper was a couple of days old but still news to him, he figured. A few people filed in and out for coffee while he ate and perused the newspaper.

He soon turned his attention to a television on the wall that was tuned to CNN, and of course, they showed "breaking news" from Ukraine. Graze had a low opinion of the cable news shows in general but was glad to see Anderson Cooper.

He considered much of Ukraine coverage to be "war porn," now complete with warnings of explicit content. The networks were in competition for millions of viewers tuning in for news of the war. He cringed when he saw some talking head in Lviv with a flak vest and plastic helmet. Those clowns reminded him of the crazy weathercasters you sometimes see, clinging to a signpost in a Florida hurricane, trying to make the six o'clock news.

Of course, he understood it was a business, and more viewers meant more advertising bucks, but war felt to Jerry like a deeply personal thing, intimate even. To his thinking, the story of the crying widow who spent three weeks in hiding, only able to exit to scavenge food by stepping over the rotting corpse of her husband . . . that doesn't belong to a TV audience thousands of miles away.

As much as Graze despised the commercialization of war by cable news, there was one possible exception in his mind—the news anchor that was on the TV now. He knew enough of Cooper's backstory to know that a silver spoon had not spared him from pain or adversity. Graze had followed him during his early years with Channel One and respected (possibly even related to) the emotional toll that the horrors of war have on a person.

Jerry had read two of Cooper's books—*Dispatches from the Edge* and *The Rainbow Comes and Goes*. The former chronicled the author's experiences over two decades following a trail of bloodshed and chaos to all corners of the world: Somalia, Bosnia, Rwanda, Afghanistan, and Iraq, as a war correspondent. Cooper related the story in his first book of the photograph that changed his life. A friend had snapped a picture of him bending over and taking pictures of rotting bloated corpses in Rwanda during the genocide.

The photo made Cooper realize that he had become so immersed in war and violence that he had lost himself. He had drunk so often from the cup of human horror that it had stopped being horrible to him. The photo is pinned to a board in Cooper's office at CNN to this day. Graze wondered once again if he should have stepped away long ago as Cooper did. Maybe the injuries that ended his career were really a blessing in disguise.

Graze pulled his thoughts back to the present and switched off the TV. Glancing at his watch, he guessed Tariq would be finished with morning prayers. He cleaned up his mess, refilled his mug, and headed up to get . . . what? Ready for church? He laughed to himself, "Haven't done that in a while."

At 0859, Graze assumed his position on the front steps, squeaky clean and smooth-shaven. He was sporting a nearly wrinkle-free black polo shirt, jeans, and his Tony Lamas, as he nervously awaited Ailana. She arrived at exactly 0900, and Jerry waved and greeted her with, "Happy Easter."

She replied with a lively, *"Wesołego Alleluja!"* As Graze climbed in, she explained that it was the proper Polish Easter greeting. Graze's parents spoke a little Polish sometimes, so Graze knew a few words. He would learn more on the ride to Warsaw.

"Wow, you clean up pretty good, Sarge."

Jerry blushed a little and replied, "Ummm . . . you ain't too bad yourself there, ma'am." He immediately felt like an idiot. The truth was, she looked fantastic. She was wearing a sleeveless cotton sundress and matching silver peace-sign earrings and necklace, and her open-toed shoes revealed brightly painted toenails. As she sped off, double clutching through the gears, he feigned interest in her fancy footwork to look over her amazing legs. As if on cue, she hitched up in her seat and tugged her dress a little more towards her knees.

The drive to Warsaw through light Easter traffic passed quickly. They listened to the radio quite a bit, and Graze was surprised that she knew all the words to Don McLean's "American Pie." She also helped him bone up on his limited Polish until he was confident in his ability to say thank you, my name is Jerry, Happy Easter, and nice to meet you, at a minimum. She was right about Oscar the Grouch. It hummed along easily at 100 kph and even had seat belts—sorta. The old Lada had low-back seats and lap belts only, like older American autos prior to 1967.

They skirted south of the city proper, crossing the wide, serene Vistula River on the Siekierkowski suspension bridge. Jerry commented that the city was quite beautiful and that he didn't know it had so many skyscrapers. Ailana pointed out one building that loomed over the others. "The Varso Tower will be open in September and is already the tallest building in the EU. You can see from the view that Warsaw has many buildings— fifteen, I think—over 150 meters."

"Yes, the city has a beautiful modern skyline, for sure."

"You will soon see that Warsaw is a city that blends the best of the old and new, Jerry."

Soon after crossing the bridge, Ailana began to wind her way north through the Praga district, pointing out various museums, markets, and other points of interest. After another ten minutes or so, she parked on a narrow street, delighted to have found a spot near her apartment. It was 1030 hrs when they climbed out of the car.

She spotted him rubbing his right leg and asked if he was up to a ten-minute walk to church. "Sure. My right leg just gets a little stiff after sitting for a while. I'm ready when you are."

She fetched a white lace shawl and a cute bonnet from the back seat. "We are going to church, after all, not a party." On the short walk, he noticed all the shops were closed, as he had suspected they would be. She paused in front of one spot to show him the PiwPaw Beer Heaven, telling him it was one of many multi-tap craft beer pubs in Warsaw and one of her favorite hangouts close to her apartment.

They soon arrived at a large open plaza brimming with people all wearing their Sunday best. The square was dominated by a beautiful gothic-style cathedral with twin towers capped by majestic bronze spires. Ailana explained that a church had been at this location for hundreds of years. The building standing before them had been originally completed in 1902 but destroyed by German forces in 1944.

As he looked up at the impressive structure, Jerry wondered aloud why the Germans, who were Christians, would destroy a church for no reason.

"Most of the city was destroyed by the Germans out of spite and hatred as they retreated. Practically everything you see in this city has been rebuilt over many years. The cathedral was rebuilt slowly, beginning in 1952 and re-opened in 1972. It is named St Florino's Cathedral after the patron saint of firefighters."

They wound their way through the square and up the steps into the church, exchanging Easter greetings with the happy crowd as they went. After the obligatory finger-dipping and signing of the cross, they found seats on a crowded pew about halfway to the front. Jerry had visited many such places over the years, and he was quite impressed with the stonework, high arching buttresses, and beautiful stained-glass windows.

Soon after seating, the priestly procession slowly came down the center aisle, complete with an ornate gold cross, ringing bells, and clanging incense. The heavy fragrance of Frankincense triggered memories of attending mass as a youngster with his family. He smiled to himself, remembering his father in church joking, "Holy Smoke!" Though Jerry didn't understand any of the spoken words in Latin and Polish, the experience otherwise was very familiar and surprisingly comforting to him, especially communion.

In less than an hour, they were back out in the sunshine of the crowded square. Ailana led Jerry towards the periphery, where several street vendors were selling various food items. She purchased a single, generous portion of schnitzel with french fries in a styrofoam to-go container, and they strolled for a few minutes until finding a vacant bench near a flower garden. As they ate lunch, she revealed their itinerary for the remainder of the day.

"When we finish our lunch, we will take an Uber across the river to see a new art exhibit called the Art Box and then return to my apartment by 1600. Some special friends of mine are preparing a nice Easter dinner." She pulled out her iPhone as Jerry polished off the remaining schnitzel and fries, and she soon announced their driver was just five minutes away. The Uber app displayed a map showing their driver's route, and the squeaky clean Toyota Corolla arrived on time. The driver was a Syrian refugee and was pleased to practice English with his riders as he maneuvered through light traffic.

About twenty minutes later, the couple was deposited in front of what appeared to be an old factory with big signs on the front in Polish and English advertising *The Art Box Experience* and *Retro Warsaw*. There was a long line of people at the entrance, and Jerry asked, "What is this place?"

Ailana held up a pretty finger to shush him as she made a short call in Polish. Finished, she explained while leading him around to the rear of the building, "The new exhibit is extremely popular and sold out months in advance, but I have a connection with one of the artists, and she will let us in through the back." Just then, a door opened, and they were ushered inside by a young Polish woman.

The two friends exchanged hugs and greetings for a few seconds until Ailana introduced her to Jerry. Teresa spoke great English and welcomed Jerry to the exhibit. She rattled off something to Ailana in Polish with a wink and raised eyebrow, which a slightly blushing Ailana ignored and inquired about the bathrooms. Teresa led them down a narrow hallway to a pair of doors with a WC placard and the universal icons of men and women. After a few minutes, the group was reunited in the hallway, and Teresa excused herself to make arrangements.

As they waited for Teresa to return, Ailana filled Jerry in on the exhibit. Reading from a small pamphlet that Teresa had given her and translating into English, she recounted "an immersive space where unique multi-sensory shows are created at the intersection of art, science, digital technology, and entertainment." It had just opened in late March and was billed as a "one-of-a-kind" experience. She continued reading: "Covering an area of eight hundred square meters, Art Box's founders decided to harness the historic confines of the 19th century Norblin Factory to use Retro Warszawa as the lead motif for their first show." Teresa returned and led them through a heavy curtain into the main exhibit hall.

The two sat on one of the randomly spaced benches, and Ailana quietly pointed out some highlights. There were no lights per se, in the exhibit, but the walls, ceiling, and floors were alive with stunning color and black and white images. The sound system played a variety of music to accompany the show, and Jerry was soon immersed—as advertised—in the stunning multi-media show.

The *Retro Warsaw* exhibit depicted all the best aspects of the Interbellum Period from 1918-1939. Post-war recovery for much of Europe was bleak and extremely difficult, but for the nation of Poland and its cities, it was a fertile time of cultural rebirth. Warsaw, in particular, notably celebrated the new lease on life that Poland gained after 100 years of occupation and tyranny by Russia, Austria, and Prussia.

They wandered from room to room, pausing to sit on the small benches scattered throughout the exhibit. The show was mesmerizing, and Jerry particularly enjoyed all the old photos of Warsaw. When the show looped back to the beginning, they slipped out through the exit and hailed another Uber.

They had over an hour to kill before dinner, so Ailana suggested they visit historic Old Town, not far away. Of course, most of the shops and businesses were closed for Easter, but they enjoyed a pleasant walking tour in the warm sunshine. Ailana was eager to get Jerry's reaction to the ArtBox experience, and the two discussed it as they walked.

"Well, Jerry, how did you like it?"

"It was awesome. I have never seen anything like that. I feel like I was in another world, literally. Please be sure to thank your friend Teresa for helping us to get it."

"I loved it also. Jerry. I'm so glad you agreed to come along today."

The two continued to chat about the exhibit, as Ailana pointed out many details of Old Town, as well. After an hour, Ailana called for another Uber ride for the trip back across the river to her apartment. They made one slight detour to the Muranów district, which was the infamous Warsaw Ghetto of World War Two. There was no time for a complete tour of the area, but they did spend a few somber, reflective minutes at the Monument to the Heroes of Warsaw in Muranów Square.

Once they were back in their Uber, it was a short trip back to Ailana's apartment, arriving around 1630. The schnitzel had been over four hours ago, and Jerry was glad to be eating soon. Ailana unlocked the Lada and retrieved a large blue IKEA bag from the rear of the car. "What you got there?"

"Easter baskets, of course."

He reached in to snag a miniature Snickers bar, and she playfully slapped his hand away, saying, "These are for my neighbors and some guests. Let's go up."

Jerry carried the bag and followed her into the front lobby. She started up the stairs to her fourth-floor flat, and he hesitated, looking around. Ailana looked back over her shoulder and said, "If you are looking for the elevator, you can forget that. Most apartments in Poland under five stories are walk-ups. It's one reason we Poles are so healthy." He followed her up the stairs and noticed that her sculpted calves certainly gave credence to the benefits of using the stairs.

When they reached the front door of her flat, a variety of

shoes and sneakers could be seen neatly lined up in the hallway. She rang her doorbell, and a few seconds later, a smiling young man appeared. They spoke briefly in Ukrainian and were summarily invited inside. The young man escorted them to the dining area of the small flat. The six people seated at the crowded table all rose to greet the newcomers with beaming smiles. Ailana translated their greetings and gave a quick biography of the family to Jerry.

It soon became obvious that Ailana had allowed a family of Ukrainian refugees to use her apartment in her absence. There was an old man who looked to be about 85, two ladies in their early fifties, he guessed, and three children. The boy was fourteen, and his two younger cousins were girls aged eleven and seven. Jerry was a little surprised and quite impressed with Ailana's generosity. The table was set with nice porcelain dinnerware and water glasses, as well as a wide selection of food items. As he took his seat next to Ailana, he said with a big smile, "This is very, very nice. Thank you for inviting me."

Ailana spoke in Ukrainian again, and the group, including Jerry, all held hands while she offered a short prayer, ending with "Amen," which everyone repeated. Then she quickly added, "Okay, *smatch neh goh!*" (Polish for *bon appétit*). The food looked and smelled fantastic to Jerry, and soon his plate was piled high with ham, duck, mountains of mashed potatoes, and all kinds of side dishes.

The meal lasted an hour while the children took delight in practicing their English with the tall American. Ailana patiently helped them from time to time when they struggled for a word. Of course, the children asked the usual questions that kids ask: Are you married? What's America like? How tall are you? Are you a cowboy? That last question elicited a few chuckles around the table, and one of the Ukrainian ladies shyly asked, "Who shot JR?"

They all laughed, and Jerry answered in a conspiratorial tone, "I think it was Sue Ellen." The 80's TV show *Dallas* was very popular around the world, and he had been asked that question more than once. His response delighted the group.

At one point, the seven-year-old seated close to Jerry pointed to his scarred head and asked, "What happens for you head, Mr. Jerry?"

The adults who understood her question started to shush her, but Jerry just looked at the girl with a big smile and said, "I had a little accident a long time ago. It's nothing, really, and it doesn't even hurt." When Ailana translated his response, it seemed to satisfy everyone, including the little girl. Ailana smiled as she segued to the big blue bag that the children had been eyeing. She handed out Easter baskets to everyone, starting with the youngest.

When she was finished, she set the bag down, and Jerry gave her a sad puppy dog look, gesturing with empty hands.

Aliana acted as if she didn't understand his questioning look for a moment, then smiled and pulled out one of the remaining baskets and handed it to him. "There you go. I saved you the one with the Snickers bars."

The adults lounged around the table after dinner drinking hot tea and sampling pastries while the children scurried off to feast on their goodies. The old man, named Borys, motioned to an empty seat next to him, and Jerry sat down, watching as the man's scarred but steady hands reached to the side table. Borys pulled a bottle of vodka and two glasses onto the table in front of him, pouring two generous shots. The two men raised their glasses in a toast and quickly drank.

Then he spoke something to the ladies present, and they quickly collected some plates and headed for the kitchen, leaving Ailana, Jerry, and Borys alone. The man then began to speak again, interrupted periodically by Ailana so she could translate. He wanted to thank Jerry for helping his country, and he wanted to introduce his family to Jerry—the family not present, the family the old man might never see again.

Borys then carefully laid out five photographs before him as he fondly touched each photo and spoke in glowing terms about his two sons and three grandsons. He continued uninterrupted, so Ailana just whispered the highlights to Jerry. Names, occupations, hobbies. A doctor this one; hunter that one; a gardener, a chef. Borys was clearly very proud of his sons and grandsons, and as he spoke, he seemed to get more emotional until his voice began to crack and give way to his trembling lips. Finally, he grew quiet and closed his eyes—perhaps to steady his nerves or to halt the flow of tears down his cheeks.

After a few deep breaths, Borys, his hands no longer steady, refilled their glasses with Vodka, tipped his glass toward Jerry, and the two downed the drinks in one large gulp. Borys seemed to ponder his empty glass for a moment, then slammed it loudly on the table as he growled in a deep guttural tone, *"Putin khuylo!"* Ailana translated it as "Screw Putin!" though Jerry was sure the phrase would have started with an "f" in English.

As Borys continued to tell the story of his family, Jerry learned that they all had lived in Kharkiev for many generations. The women with Borys in Poland were the wives of his two married sons, who had remained in Ukraine along with Borys's three grandsons to fight the Russians. The children with Borys were his great-grandchildren.

The wives of his grandsons had refused to leave Kharkiev, volunteering instead to take up arms and support their husbands. One of the women had called two weeks ago with news that all five of the men had been sent to the front lines in the east. No one had heard from any of them since that day.

Borys poured two more shots but placed his hand over

the top of them and leaned in close, and spoke softly to Jerry in Ukrainian. "Look at me, Jerry." This time he allowed Ailana to translate. "I have been a soldier, and I have killed and seen war. I know a soldier when I see one. I know a killer when I see one. I don't believe you are here to move boxes around. I think you are here to kill Russians."

He lifted a glass to Jerry then and raised his own. "Drink with me one last time, but only if you promise to do your job well and do it quickly. I want to see my family again."

The man waited with his own glass poised to drink and warily eyed the American until Jerry tossed back the drink and slammed the glass on the table, saying, *"Putin khuylo!"* Satisfied, Borys finished his drink also and set the bottle back on the side table, for which Jerry was silently grateful. He was already feeling light-headed and doubted he could keep pace with the old man much longer.

Soon thereafter, Ailana started making her way towards the door over the chorus of objections. She prevailed by reminding them of the long drive back to the base and a busy day of work tomorrow. There were hugs around, and goodbyes, thank yous, and Happy Easters. On the way to the stairs, she left the three remaining baskets in front of select apartment doors and neatly folded the IKEA bag for future use.

Jerry guessed he'd had at least eight ounces of vodka, and he was more than a little wobbly but managed to get down the stairs and out to the car without falling. Once belted into the Lada, they wound their way out of the city and onto Rt 21 westbound. The two friends chatted about the events of the day as they traveled—the beautiful church service, the Art Box, and Easter dinner with the Ukrainian family. Jerry told her that he had a wonderful time and was grateful for the invitation.

However, when she asked what he thought of Borys, he frowned and grew sullen. The poignant story of the man's family torn apart by war and the fear they might all be dead had hit him hard. Jerry was also disturbed by the old man's ominous judgment of him as a killer. "You know, the old man is right. I am a soldier, and I have killed many men."

Ailana thought for a second before answering. "You *were* a soldier, and you have killed in war. I know this, but that was before, Jerry. People change and gain new ways of seeing life. You are a good man, and you are doing a good thing here in Poland to help the Ukrainians. That doesn't make you a killer."

Jerry shook his head slowly and let out a deep sigh before answering in a somber tone. "Oh, Ailana, if only your words were the true words, but I felt the old man's eyes drilling deep into my soul, and he saw who I really am."

"Oh, Jerry, Borys doesn't know anything about you, really. You have had a lot to drink, so try to get a nap now, ok?" They were both silent after that, and once they crossed the suspension bridge, the steady drone of the tires soon lulled Jerry into a drunken sleep.

He awoke in front of the barracks to Ailana gently shaking him. "Okay, party pooper, it's time to get up. We are home."

It was just past 1900 hrs, and Tariq was sitting on the steps with earphones listening to music and soaking in the last of the fading sunshine. He rushed over when he saw Ailana struggling to extract Graze from the car. "Hey, what's going on? Is Jerry okay?"

"Oh, he will be fine. We had a great day in Warsaw, but Jerry may have had one too many glasses of vodka."

Tariq reached in and pulled his friend onto his feet. "Ah, man, what did you do?" Then to Ailana, "I got him from here. We will see you in the morning. Thanks for getting him home."

"Cool, man. Make sure he takes some ibuprofen or tylenol tonight. We all have a busy day tomorrow."

Chapter 9: Dnipro

The next day, Monday, Graze was up at the usual time, albeit with a pounding headache. He and Tariq biked over to the hangar at 0715, and Graze had his third cup of coffee while Ailana finished her morning briefing. The two men stood on the opposite side of the crowded room from her as she spoke. Tariq gave Graze a nudge and whispered with a smile, "Your girlfriend looks nice today. Do you wanna move closer?" Graze just gave him a sideways glance and shuffled a few inches away from his friend.

Afterwards, Ailana was swamped by team members needing assistance, so he and Tariq slipped out the back to the van where Mark and the Dagger crew were already waiting. The ibuprofen and black coffee did their magic on Graze's head, and by the time they reached the training grounds, he was ready to rock and roll. The Dagger was silently awaiting them, silhouetted by the rising sun and poised ominously for action.

The NCOs, of course, lit up cigarettes, and they all enjoyed fruit-filled *Pączkis* and coffee from two large thermos jugs that the driver unloaded. Mark asked the men to have a seat at the picnic tables while he briefed them on the modifications to the Dagger. Tariq and Graze sat together away from the chain-smoking Ukrainians, as usual. Neither men complained about the habit but kept their distance when possible. While they waited for Mark to get started, Tariq quietly grilled his friend on his date with Ailana.

"Number one. It was *not* a date," stated Graze.

"Come on, man. It's me. I can tell you like her, and it seems like she really likes you, too. What did you guys do, anyhow, and how come only you got drunk last night?"

"Okay, it was a great day. Warsaw is an amazing city, and believe it or not, I really enjoyed going to church."

"That's cool, bro. I'm glad you went to talk to God."

"Shush now. Mark is about to start. I promise to give you all the details later."

The first order of business was for Mark to go over the new modifications that had been completed on Sunday. They followed him over to the Dagger as he spoke. He showed them that a small door had been added to the floor of the troop compartment near the rear left door. It was a little over twelve inches square and hinged on the front. When opened, it swung down, making a sort of ramp or slide that reached to the ground below. Aleksandr climbed in and operated the mechanism, which dropped the door open. "Great, now we don't have to stop to use the toilet."

Mark laughed. "Well, I didn't think of that, as that's not the primary purpose."

He pointed out a small rack installed beneath the troop seats. There were four metal discs stored, each about a foot in diameter and four inches tall. Pavel recognized them immediately. "Aha, Russian TM-46 anti-tank mines— reliable and deadly."

"Good boy!" Pete said. "The idea here is that when you are being pursued by enemy vehicles, you can open this door and drop one or two of the mines. Of course, these four mines are inert for training and have strobes attached to locate them after use. The real ones will be found by others using the exploding method." Mark demonstrated to the team how to remove the mines from storage and use them. Each mine had a six-foot lanyard attached to the arming mechanism to allow the mine to be safely deployed.

The crew took a few minutes to familiarize themselves with the mines, after which Mark went on with the briefing. "The Dagger has also been given a shot of adrenaline. Finland owns many of the same model and version of BMP-2 as do the Ukrainians. About five years ago, they retrofitted their vehicles by adding an exhaust gas turbine. The modification increases the power from 300 HP to 375, and the higher RPMs increase the maximum road speed to around 75 kph. Over the weekend, their team added the same turbine to your machine."

"Do we need training for this?" Aleksandr asked.

"Yes, I almost forgot to say there is a new switch in the driver's compartment labeled TURBO, with a red light next to the switch that lights up when the turbo is operating. Use it sparingly, as it increases fuel consumption by about fifteen percent.

"One more change is also from our friends in Finland. A proprietary passive thermal cloaking system has been installed in the engine's compartment and the exhaust system that reduces thermal radiation by sixty to seventy percent."

Tariq looked at his friend with crazy eyes, and Graze shook his head slowly. "Don't . . . don't say it . . ."

Tariq held his breath for about five seconds, then blurted out, "We got a freaking cloaking device! Dude, we are KLINGONS!" The enlisted Ukrainians instantly caught the reference and also thought it was hilarious. The *Star Trek* franchise was very popular in Ukraine, and they all knew who Klingons were. As soon as they settled down and stopped chuckling, Mark continued with his briefing. He got about three words out when Pavel interrupted in his best Captain Kirk accent, "Scotty, three to beam up!" The men instantly exploded again, laughing so hard they were crying. Mark just shook his head but couldn't help smiling. "Okay, guys, let's settle down."

They eventually got back to work, though there were several random Star Trek quotes on the intercom throughout the day, usually in a Scottish accent. Joking aside, the crew spent a long day of active training. Before lunch, they practiced loading, prepping, and firing Big Birds and

Tweeties from a moving vehicle into the target pit, as well as launch and recovery of the RQ-11 Raven reconnaissance drone. The four-pound Raven would provide important real-time imagery during the planned mission, having a ten-km range and flight time of ninety minutes.

In the afternoon, the crew practiced with the mines and the radar system to detect and track airborne targets, courtesy of an unsuspecting nearby civilian airport. As usual, the men would trade positions throughout the day, with the exception of Graze, who stayed in the mission commander's compartment at all times.

As soon as lunch finished, Mark caught a ride to Warsaw again on the newest helicopter of the Polish Marine Corps. The sleek craft was the first of five EH-101s purchased by Poland from the firm Agustawestland. The Marine unit operating them in Poland was equivalent to the U.S. Marine Squadron HMX-1, and like its American counterpart, the mission was VIP transport.

Mark knew that many nations around the world utilized the EH-101 for their "Presidential Helicopter." In fact, Mark was aware that the United States tried to procure them to replace the 45-year-old Sikorsky VH-3D Sea King, but the contract was an utter failure. After investing five years and billions of dollars, the contract tripped congressional overrun thresholds for the second time in 2008 and was canceled the following year. Riding now in the beautiful craft, Mark just shook his head with regret that the U.S. Marines did not have them.

The Dagger crew finished for the day around 1800 and headed back to the base. Mark had called Pete earlier to say he would be in Warsaw late and would see them all in the morning. On Tuesday morning, Mark met the crew as usual to oversee their training, though Graze noticed an increased sense of urgency in his former commander. At lunch, Graze asked, "So, any news from the honchos in Warsaw? Are we still a go?"

"Right now, I can say that the Russians are still continuing to retreat from Kiev and regroup in the east of Ukraine. We have just a couple of days now to train for the Dagger mission. What's your assessment, Gunny? Is the team ready to launch?"

"We are getting there, boss. The old BMP is performing much better than I had expected, and the crew is working very well together. Two more days of hard training should do it."

"Good. Finish your lunch and hit it hard."

The Dagger crew practiced every aspect of the planned mission virtually around the clock, for the next two days. At lunch Thursday, Mark met the crew at the practice range but sat apart from the group, conferring with Pete and Graze quietly. The other men had not been briefed on the exact details of Operation Sunflower yet but sensed a big announcement was coming.

When they had finished eating, Pete gathered all the men around and began to speak. "Men, I am very, very proud of you all. You have been training hard night and day for a solid week, and your teamwork and skills are impressive. The Dagger is ready, and *you* are ready." General Smirnov paused then and looked each man in the eye with a solemn expression. Then in a loud voice, he enthusiastically announced, "Men, it is time to go to war. We leave tonight!" After a brief pause, all the men burst into shouts and applause.

Mark allowed them to celebrate for a few minutes, then corralled them into the van for the ride back to the base. Mark and Pete briefed the crew on the details of the planned mission during the 45-minute drive. As soon as they arrived, Mark led the crew through the office into the locked conference room.

The first thing they all noticed were large boxes of freshly laundered used Russian uniforms and equipment. Pete invited the men to each find a uniform and boots that fit. As the crew dug through the boxes, Aleksandr held up a tunic with two fingers poking through small round holes. "Hey, where did you get these uniforms? Most seem to have holes in them."

Pete answered with a grin, "Let's just say they were donated by Russian soldiers who don't need them anymore, okay?"

After an hour of trial and error, each of the crew members were dressed in Russian uniforms and stood for inspection. Each man was then issued a Russian ballistic vest, helmet, dog tags, and fake ID cards. Satisfied with their disguises, Pete led them to a table where the standard-issue Russian MP-443 "Grach" 9 mm pistol and AK-74 assault rifle were lying. He gave a quick tutorial on the features, cleaning, and disassembly of the weapons. When finished, he told them, "Now, please put everything into the duffle bag marked with your name and get dressed again. These bags will be waiting for you in the Dagger, along with everything else for the mission."

They finished up by 1700, and Mark dismissed them. "Okay, men, get some chow and some sleep if you can. The van will be picking you up at midnight." They were also reminded of the secrecy of the mission and ordered to speak of it to no one. The cover story, if needed, was that they were traveling to another base in Poland for a few days to help with a different project. In reality, the six crew members would travel by train to Kiev with their vehicle and begin the mission to lead the counter-offensive.

After dinner that evening, Ailana dropped by the barracks to see Jerry. "I heard you are going up to the Baltic for a few days. There are some great beach areas around Gdansk if you have any free time." They talked for a while, and at one point, Ailana lamented that they wouldn't be able to continue his Polish lessons.

"Yes, I have learned better Polish for sure, but maybe I should have learned Russian instead." As soon as the words came out of his mouth, he knew he had screwed up.

Ailana stared ahead for a few seconds, thinking. "Why Russian? Why would you need to speak Russian?" He tried to blow it off, saying he was only joking.

She shook her head and shouted, "Bullshit, Jerry! Do you think I am stupid? Do you think I haven't seen the Russian markings on that tank you are training on or the Russian uniforms in the conference room?" Before Jerry could respond, she stormed back to her car, opened the door, and shouted back over the roof, "I know Mark and that Ukrainian general have dreamed up some kind of crazy mission. They are going to get you killed, Jerry, and WHY? Why do it? It's not your war!"

He walked over to the car, locking eyes with Ailana. "I'm sorry, but the old man in your apartment was right about me, no matter how much we want to believe differently." He turned and walked back to the front door of the barracks, silently hoping she would stop him, but she sped off in anger.

When he got up to his room, he and Tariq packed all of their personal items into B-4 bags, put on fresh clothes, and tried to get some shut-eye. Sleep had not come to either man when the clock radio sounded the alarm at 2330 hrs. The two grabbed coffee and found the van was waiting outside with the rest of the crew. Everyone was dead quiet on the short ride to the hangar, where Mark was waiting to lead them into the conference room for a pre-departure briefing.

The group sat at the large conference table, where some supplies had been set out. "Good morning, gentlemen. Please place all your personal items, including wallets, keys, cell phones, and photos, into the plastic zip lock bags on the table. There is also a paper tag and some pens for each of you. Write your name and the contact information of relatives on the tag and seal it in the Ziplock with your things."

Graze naturally put his sister's information on the tag, and when the men were all finished, the bags were placed into a wooden crate, along with their luggage. The crate was unmarked except for two sunflower decals. As Mark nailed the lid on the box, he explained, "This box will be kept secure in the Cave here and returned to you when you return, or . . ." Mark let the sentence trail off as he drove the final nail and carefully set the hammer down.

Then Mark led the six men of the Dagger crew out into the darkness to a nearby railroad siding. Waiting for them was one oddly large passenger car attached to an idling diesel locomotive. The men assumed that another flatbed rail car with the Dagger would be added to the train, but that was not the case. After boarding through the forward door of the train car, it was immediately obvious that the rear two-thirds of the passenger car had been gutted to make room for their BMP, which was chained to the floor.

The crew took a few minutes to inspect the interior of their new home away from home. Tariq said, "This reminds me of one of the ships in a bottle. How was this done?"

Pete explained, "The rear end of the rail car has been cut off and bolted back on after the BMP was loaded. When you arrive in Dnipro in a few days, the process will be reversed. The antennas, radar mast, and other items had to be removed for transport, so two Ukrainian technicians will travel with you to reassemble the Dagger and perform operational checks in Dnipro."

The men were all impressed with the effort to camouflage the train for the trip to Kiev. The smaller front section of the rail car had eight large, comfortably padded bench seats. Since they would be living in the train car for nearly three full days, the designers had been careful to provide the necessities of life, including a lavatory, shower, and small kitchen area with a cook stove, microwave, and well–stocked refrigerator.

After the crew finished examining the contents of the specially modified car, they all took a seat while Mark gave final instructions. "The trip through Lviv and onto Kiev will take approximately sixteen hours, during which time you will not be leaving the train. This car has been disguised as an ordinary passenger car to fool Russian spies and satellite imagery, as the Russians monitor all traffic from Poland to Ukraine. In fact, you eight men are the only passengers on the train. Everything for the mission, including your uniforms and weapons, are already loaded into the Dagger.

"The other barges of the flotilla are being loaded now with the tanks, helicopters, Air Defense systems, soldiers, and supplies needed to establish the new base in Dnipro. This special train car will be loaded onto a barge in Kiev and begin the 45-hour journey down the Dnieper River. Before arriving at the port, you men will don your Russian disguises and be the first unit to unload."

Mark further explained that a Ukrainian army patrol would escort them from Dnipro 230 km to the rear area of the Ukrainian front lines outside Donetsk. From there, they would be on their own to covertly cross 35-40 km of no man's land, penetrate the Russian lines, and move into attack position.

At exactly 45 minutes past midnight, the train engineer gave two short blasts on the air horn, which was Mark's signal to make for the door. He shook hands with each man and wished them good luck and Godspeed. As the train started to move, Mark whispered to Graze, "I'll be waiting in Dnipro for you when you return. As soon as you get clear of

Russian-controlled territory, contact me, and I will pick you up. Good luck, Gunny."

"*Semper Fi.*"

"*Oorah.*"

Most of the men soon fell asleep on the comfortable benches until prodded awake by the sunlight and aroma of freshly brewed coffee. Soon the seven men were sipping coffee at the dining table while Pavel prepared eggs and sausage.

After breakfast, the men relaxed as best they could manage. The Ukrainian NCOs convinced Pete to allow them to smoke with a window open, so they played cards and dominos for most of the time while chain-smoking. The other men played chess on a small magnetic chess set produced by Tariq. The general and Tariq played first, and Graze smiled to himself when Tariq opened with the King's Gambit, and black accepted the "free" pawn. During his two years in Afghanistan, Graze had played hundreds of chess games with his Afghani friend on that very same board. Whenever Tariq played white, he always opened with that move. Predictably, Pete soon found himself in deep trouble defending against the withering attacks on his king.

The boredom of the trip was interrupted briefly when their train reached Lviv, where they changed engines for the final leg to Kiev. Their train had stopped just outside the main station there, affording a clear view of crowds on the platforms. Looking out the windows, Pavel was the first to comment. *"Bozhe miy!* Look how many people are arriving from the east!" The others quickly joined Pavel at the windows, and Pete added, "Refugees - thousands of women and children running from the murderous Russians!" Look carefully, men, and remember that this is the reason we must not fail." All the men continued to watch the crowds until their train left for Kiev.

They were expected to arrive in Kiev by 1800, so the group snacked through lunch and ate dinner early at 1600. By the time they were cleaning up, the train was slowly crawling through the suburbs of Kiev. Graze was looking out a window at the rain that had started to fall. Pete came along and slapped him on the back. "Yes, rain is good. Rain is very good. It makes it hard for our Russian friends above to see us."

Pavel was looking out the window as well, and Graze asked him, "Kiev is your hometown, correct?"

"Yes, sir." He pointed to the northwest, where the sky was lit by the orange glow of fires. "My home is just over in that direction, actually. There was a Russian cruise missile attack in that area yesterday, with many reported deaths. Part of me wants to jump out this window and run to my family."

Graze could hear the pain and fear in the man's voice and placed his hand on his shoulder and solemnly said, "I promise we will do our best to punish the bastards who are doing this and that soon you will see your family again, Pavel."

"I believe the first thing you say, but only God can keep them safe for now. With all my heart, I wish I could be there to protect them." Graze started to speak again, but the man quickly added, "Yes, my friend, we *will* do our best, and we will *not* fail."

Instead of going into the Central Train Station in Kiev, the train took a series of smaller lines and slowly made its way onto a siding in the warehouse district south of the city, finally coming to a stop. The crew disembarked, realizing they were very near to a service canal leading to the Dnieper River a mile away. A line of barges was tied up along the canal, all with tarps and other covers, making them look like farm equipment and grain barges. The engine disconnected from their car and reconnected with another outwardly identical car for the twenty-minute ride to the city center. The Russian spies who monitored all train traffic would not easily detect the deception.

While the crew watched, a small tractor slowly inched their car onto a waiting barge. There were already seven railcars with tanks and missile systems loaded, and the Dagger car was the last on and would be the first off in Dnipro.

As soon as the barge was loaded and secured, the crew of the Dagger returned to their car, and a heavy tarp was pulled over them for camouflage. They were joined by three other canal boats, and a powerful tug began to push the boats toward the river at just past 2000 hrs. With any luck, they would arrive in Dnipro in 46 hours.

The crew passed the time talking together and playing cards. Tariq became quite good at the card game *durak* and was soon collecting a fair share of the wagers. *Durak* (meaning *fool* in Russian) originated in that country and was immensely popular in Russia and Ukraine. Graze spent most of his free time in the mission command compartment of the Dagger, studying intelligence reports and satellite imagery. Before leaving Poland, Colonel Stapelton had given him a USB jump drive with all the details of their planned mission. Graze decided to share the information with the crew once they were behind enemy lines.

Time passed slowly for the 1500 men and women on the barges during the trip downriver. The rain let up after the first four hours of travel, but they were forbidden to open the canopies to enjoy the sunshine for security reasons. Nevertheless, the next morning Aleksandr and Dmytryi managed to roll up a few feet of cover at the rear of the barge, letting the morning sun onto an open space in front of their train car.

When Pete found the men sitting on crates eating breakfast, his first reaction was to scold them and order them back to the car, but he thought better of it. Instead, he checked with Graze over the intercom for any reports of Russian drones in the area. After conferring with Graze about the breach of security, the two decided to allow the crew an hour of sunshine. Soon the entire crew was basking in the morning light. Pete and Graze spoke quietly out of earshot from the rest of the crew.

"Do you think they are ready?" Graze asked.

Pete surveyed the men joking and smoking for a few seconds. "Yes. They have become a very close team and well-practiced for the action that awaits us. They know the risks, and I believe the sight of all the refugees in Lviv has hardened their resolve. Let them enjoy the sunshine for now."

The tow continued without incident down the wide, lazy river, arriving at a port facility near Dnipro at 1830 hrs on Sunday evening. As planned, the mission car was unloaded first and guided onto a siding nearby. The technicians, with local help, rapidly unbolted the rear of the passenger car, and the BMP was driven out into the gathering dusk. Forty minutes later, the Dagger was fully assembled and declared operational. The six men, having donned their Russian disguises, then took their places in the Dagger.

Pete was satisfied that the vehicle and systems were ready. He moved the vehicle about a quarter mile to the designated rendezvous spot where a Ukrainian BTR-60 was waiting for them. They were greeted by four Ukrainian soldiers, led by a barrel-chested captain smoking a stubby cigar. Pete jumped down amid mumbled comments by the BTR crew, who had noticed Pete's Russian officer's uniform.

Graze joined the men in discussing the next phase of the operation. The Ukrainian captain explained that their vehicle would take the lead. He had confidence that the roads leading east were in Ukrainian control, and they would stay on blacktop roads for much of the 235 kilometers to the Ukrainian front lines. It was agreed to maintain complete radio silence during the four- to five-hour trip. The captain then handed Pete a black disc, a little bigger than a hockey puck, with a small glass dome on top. He explained that it was an infrared strobe that could be programmed to pulse in dots and dashes—Morse Code.

The captain showed the two how to turn it on and program the device easily. He told Pete, "The device has been pre-loaded to emit the code for 'stop.' You are to attach the magnetic base of the strobe on the turret visible to the lead vehicle, as ours will be. There are three Ukrainian checkpoints on the route, which will be alerted as we approach with our strobe transmitting prearranged passwords."

When Pete and Graze returned to the Dagger, they found the crew stretching their legs and smoking outside the vehicle. Pete said with a clap of his hands, "Okay, men, let's load up. We are gonna be in this can for the next five hours. If you need to piss, now is the time."

Aleksandr hopped into the back and said, "No worries, sir. We have a urinal back here, remember?"

Pete waved him inside with a smile.

The next five hours were uneventful as the small convoy moved quickly through the pitch-black, moonless night. Two bridges had been destroyed by Russian jets along the route, which caused slight delays. In one case, the Ukrainians had set up a pontoon bridge nearby, and the other required fording a shallow stream. They were ushered through the checkpoints with cheers from the Ukrainian soldiers.

At 0130, the convoy was met by an American-built M114 Humvee. Graze, of course, recognized the squat four-wheeled workhorse of the U.S. military but was surprised to find one in Ukraine. When he questioned Pete on the intercom, Pete told him, "These are more goodies from the Americans. We have nearly 200, um . . . I should say *had.*'"

The Humvee led them to a small command post, where they shut down and climbed out, stretching and groaning from the five-hour ride. While the men unwound (and smoked, of course), Graze and Pete were ushered into a mobile command post parked under a nearby tree. The colonel who greeted them inside was obviously a friend of Pete's, and the two hugged and spoke in rapid-fire

Ukrainian. Graze was introduced, and the three men settled around a single table with a satellite terminal and several maps on it. While the colonel logged on, he spoke again in Ukrainian to General Smirnov, to which Pete nodded, getting up to pour three cups of hot, black coffee.

The Ukrainian colonel began his briefing. "As you can see by the timestamp, this imagery is about two hours old, but we believe it is still accurate. The analysts in Kiev have edited the image by adding critical information that you will need." He zoomed in on the area between their current position and the city of Donetsk, approximately 65 km to the east. The map allowed the three to study checkpoints, minefields, and terrain in no man's land between the Ukrainian and Russian lines. Their planned route would take approximately three hours, putting them at the Russian lines at approximately 0400—*if* everything went well.

Using a color stylus on the touch screen, the three mapped out the most covert route using farm tracks, streams, and forested areas to cross to the Russian front lines. They were careful to mark Ukrainian minefields but had only guesses about any Russian mines. The weather forecast, confirmed on radar, was for a line of thunderstorms ahead along their route that would help provide cover for them.

After about thirty minutes, Graze and Pete thanked the colonel and went outside to discover the vehicle had been refueled and thoroughly inspected by the crew. The six men retired to a little mess tent and ate lentil soup with dense, dark bread and coffee. While they ate, Graze briefed the crew on the basics of the plan. They would proceed alone east along back roads and tree lines under cover of rain for the first two hours. When the rain let up, they would launch the "eye in the sky" RQ-11 drone and proceed to a location two km from a Russian checkpoint. Pete would make radio contact with the Russians using the "logistics guys" cover story and fake orders. With a lot of luck, they would be behind enemy lines by 0400, giving them three hours to reach the launch point for the Big Birds.

When the men returned to the Dagger, they were met by the unit chaplain offering confession and a blessing. The men all passed on the confession but agreed to accept a sprinkling and a prayer. When the chaplain left, Dmytryi announced, "It is good to get the blessings from the God of Peace, but let's all call upon the gods of war to be with us as well." He pulled out six small tin cups and a bottle of vodka from his pack and passed them out, filling each one to the top. He then offered his own prayer in English: "We drink to the gods of war and death. We call upon them to go with us and before us, wreaking death and revenge on the demons that have killed our families and destroyed our land. May the God of Peace have mercy on all our souls." Three minutes later, they were gone, disappearing into the quiet night as the first drops of rain began to fall. The time was 0130.

Chapter 10: The Dagger

The Dagger stealthily crept across no man's land for the next two hours, mostly under the cover of rain. The normally talkative, light-hearted chatter was replaced by an eerie silence, interrupted periodically by Pete over the intercom with instructions to the driver. Pete kept the Dagger on farm tracks and abandoned rail beds as much as possible. Using the radar, Graze kept a sharp eye out for Russian drones and other aircraft. The rain let up at 0330, and Pete released an RQ-11 Raven drone minutes afterwards. They were within ten km of the Russian lines, and the crew carefully monitored the drone imagery until they found the checkpoint for which they were looking.

At 0402 hrs, the Dagger came to a stop approximately two km from the Russian position and shut down. Graze toggled the drone's sensors from EO to thermal and was easily able to assess the enemy defenses. Stanchions with barbed wire were stretched across the road, and he noticed two sandbagged fighting positions at the far corners of the intersection. He also spotted two T-80 tanks as well as two BTR-80s with 30 mm autocannons on the far side of the intersection.

Pete gave a low whistle and said, "That is a lot of firepower. Is there any chance to sneak around these guys?"

In response, Graze guided the drone north and then south, looking for an opening, but squads of dismounted infantry and armored vehicles were scattered on the farm tracks and wheat fields every kilometer. After a few minutes of reconnaissance, Pete conceded that it was too risky to bypass the checkpoint.

Graze guided the silent drone back over the roadblock for a closer look. Pete said, "Based on the thermals, none of the vehicles are running, though they may be crewed and could start up at any time. Each of the BTRs can carry ten troops, so it is likely that there are perhaps twenty to thirty men sleeping in the tents near their position. What do you think, Graze?"

"We are running out of time. We don't have another option, so I say we talk our way past these guys. It's up to you now, *Major Ivansko.*"

Pete got on the intercom and apprised the entire crew. He gave the particulars of the checkpoint two klicks ahead, along with the other enemy positions. After a brief discussion, it was agreed they would have to bluster their way past the Russian position on the road ahead of them. Pete said into the intercom, "Okay, my friends, game time. Everyone, keep your heads down and mouths shut. I'm gonna put in the call. Let's get ready to roll."

Pete then keyed the mic and transmitted on open radio in Russian: "This is Major Ivansko, attached to 24th Combat

Logistics Battalion, calling Russian checkpoint at mile marker 203. Please respond." They all waited as the radio remained silent.

Pete keyed the mic again and repeated his call. This time a youngish voice answered. "This is Lieutenant Kirkov of the Russian Army. What is your position, and what is your purpose here?" The lieutenant was probably surprised to be contacted at this hour of the morning, and Pete could detect the caution in his voice.

This was the moment of truth. The mission would succeed or fail in the next few minutes. Pete cleared his throat and steadied his nerves before answering. "We are approximately two to three km west of your position on Rt #167. We are traveling under orders from Kharkiv to Amvrosiivka airport east of here. We are a single BMP logistics vehicle with parts and material for urgent helicopter repair actions."

"Very well," responded the lieutenant. "Drive forward with your lights on until I order you to stop."

From the drone footage, the men could see that one of the T-80 tanks had immediately started up its powerful turbine engine, and several figures could be seen running towards the BTRs. Four minutes later, as they approached the barricade, a blinding searchlight on top of the T-80 switched on, accompanied by a loudspeaker blaring in Russian: "Halt! Turn off your motor!" Pete was the only crewmember that could be seen happily waving, though all six men were holding their breath in anticipation.

Pete climbed down with his biggest smile and a small backpack. The young lieutenant who spoke earlier on the radio approached the side of the Dagger, barking, "You, Major Ivansko, are extremely far out of your way. All movements from the north were to be in the rear areas. You are lucky you were not shot to pieces or hit a mine."

Pete asked in his most contrite Russian for forgiveness, explaining they were in a hurry. Pete handed over a small stack of papers with their fake orders on top. "Look for yourself. It says EXPEDITE and 'make all haste.' We were delayed in traffic near Kharkiv and decided to take the shortcut. I apologize for interrupting your morning, truly, but my boss is a real ball-buster, so we had to try to make up time. You understand, I hope."

The lieutenant then eyed the old BMP and said, "I'm surprised this piece of junk made it down here at all."

Pete laughed his most friendly laugh. "Well, we are a logistics unit. We always get the leftovers, so that you fighting men can have the best of the best."

"What is so important that you are delivering?" the lieutenant inquired.

Pete then slapped the young officer on the back and headed towards the rear of the vehicle. "Look for yourself.

Boxes of parts and equipment. We are just delivery boys."

When they reached the rear of the Dagger, out of sight from the other Russians, Pete said to the lieutenant, "Look, we are supply guys, and we have access to certain small luxuries. Let me make you a present to honor your heroic duty here." Pete handed the backpack he was carrying to the lieutenant, whose eyes grew large with pleasant surprise when he looked inside. The lieutenant slung the pack over his shoulder and handed Pete back his orders.

Kirkov then announced in a loud official-sounding voice, "Very well, Major. Everything is in order. Please continue your important supply mission." The Russian officer signaled to a couple of young conscripts to move the barricade, and the Dagger rolled into Russian-controlled territory at 0415 hours on Monday, April 25th. They were now behind enemy lines, and the Dagger inched closer to the great bear's cold heart.

The crew were all sweating bullets as the Dagger rolled east away from the checkpoint. The RQ-11 drone was still up, but its battery was running low. Graze scanned around them and found a partially destroyed farmhouse four klicks ahead near the road. After a brief exchange on the intercom, Pete ordered the driver to accelerate to fifty kph until they reached the farmhouse, where they came to a stop next to the building. On Graze's control pad, the red *BATTERY LOW* light was blinking angrily as he swooped the drone down towards a grassy spot behind the building and selected "auto land" mode. Two minutes later, the lightweight drone was partially dismantled and stored in the Dagger while its battery was recharging.

The six men dismounted, and the enlisted Ukrainians all lit cigarettes while they scrounged firewood. The spot they chose had appealed to other campers, as evidenced by the amount of trash scattered around. Some rocks were piled into a rudimentary fire pit, and there were a few plastic buckets and folding chairs in the area. Tariq, Graze, and Pete found seats and gathered around an overturned plastic bucket.

The men started a small fire and retrieved MREs, water, and a small tea kettle from the Dagger and ate in silence for a few minutes as the teapot simmered on the flames. All six gathered then around Graze while he tapped the screen to wake up the display, pulling up the annotated map they had created earlier. He pinched the screen with two fingers zooming the picture to one-mile range. The computer updated and displayed a blinking blue dot in the middle of the screen, next to a ruined farmhouse. This was their current location.

"Okay," said Graze, "So far, so good. We are behind enemy lines, and in a few hours, we will begin our attack. It's time to lay our cards on the table."

One of the Ukrainian scouts asked something, and his fellow soldier could be heard saying in English: "Lay cards on table, like when we play *durak*. Time to show your cards." He looked at Pete as if to ask if that was right and was met with a nod.

Graze continued, "You all know our mission is to attack two primary targets and a third if possible."

The men nodded, and Pavel said, "Yes, we know. A command post and S-400 building. Plus, the airport, maybe, also."

"Correct, but there is more to say about the command post. You know now that a new general has taken over the Russian offensive on Ukraine."

One of the men spoke his name with disgust: "Aleksandr Dvornikov!"

Pete added, "Yes, the Butcher of Chechnya and Syria is now in command." The four Ukrainians all spat into the fire and cursed his name. "But not for long," added Pete with a wry grin.

Graze entered some keystrokes switching the map view to an area about eighty km northeast of their current position. "Target #1: General Aleksandr Dvornikov."

The Ukrainian NCOs reacted in surprise at the idea of killing this beast. Pete added some icing on the cake for them. "Not just the pig Dvornikov, but his entire murderous staff. Every senior officer under his command down to battalion level will be having breakfast this morning with the soon-to-be-dead general."

Graze explained that Dvornikov was a well-known figure with a huge ego who loved to make a show to his officers. "He is assembling his staff to announce the full-scale assault on eastern Ukraine, which we have learned is to begin tomorrow. As in the past, the general is staging something of a pep rally this morning at 0730 hrs."

Aleksandr asked, "What is *pop really?*" The question gave Graze a smile as he explained to the NCOs that a pep rally was a party held by American students before a big sports match.

Graze zoomed in on a trailer complex, just eighty km from their current position, and pointed out the large canopies and chairs set up near his command post. "As part of the event, the Russian general has brought in some newly deployed or developmental weapons systems for show-and-tell." The men could see a large, tarp-covered vehicle at the venue. "He loves to show off the latest equipment to his troops. If he stays true to form, he is expected to give a rousing ten-minute speech and then make the big reveal while soaking in the applause and cheers of his commanders."

Pavel asked, "Do we know for sure about this party and the general?"

Pete answered the question in English. "Ukrainian intelligence has a reliable spy in the general's camp who has confirmed all of these details. It is a near certainty that at 0730, we will have approximately a ten-minute window to carry out our attack, and if we succeed, it will be a great victory for our army."

As Graze adjusted the map display, he took up the briefing. "So that's target #1—we kill Dvornikov along with most of his staff, plus we destroy the 'mystery machine.' We have less than three hours to get within forty km of the command post to launch the Big Birds. Now let's look at target #2."

On the screen, the men could all see a blinking red dot approximately sixty km from the command post. Graze zoomed in for his eager audience and showed them a complex of vans and trailers. "This is the Command and Control Center for the entire southern arm of the S-400 Air Defense Network. The distance between #1 and #2 is 63 km, so we have to get to a location from which we can hit both targets at once." He drew a small circle on the screen with his stylus and centered the display on showing the area in detail.

A small deserted village along a dirt road could be seen. "This will be our initial launch point, approximately forty km from where we are now. We expect heavy Russian activity in the area, but the village itself is of no real interest to the Russians. There is nothing there but a few starving dogs and rats now. If we can get to a point either near or in this village, we will be in striking range of both targets one and two."

Pavel interrupted, "This information is several hours old. What if there are Russians there to greet us?"

Pete answered, "We will fly the Raven ahead of our travel and make sure we find a quiet place to launch. Any place within a few klicks of the village will work."

Graze agreed, "Yes, that's right. The drones can fly for forty minutes, and from anywhere near the village, it will take less than 25 minutes to reach the two targets. That will allow the Big Birds to circle the targets at 10,000 ft until we are ready to attack."

Pavel said with a smile, "So we shoot the Birds up at 0700, and thirty minutes later, the fat pig and his officers are dead? Very nice!"

Graze answered, "That's the plan, Stan, but—"

"Who is Stan?

"Nevermind . . . just American slang. As I was about to say, the plan will take fast work once we reach our launch position. While we travel, you two in the back will need to verify that all of the Big Birds are fully charged and ready to deploy. Follow your training, and get it right, men. When we are in position, get the first four mounted on the turret, then immediately load the next four after launch. If luck is on our side, we will strike both targets simultaneously around 0730 hours."

Alex and the other NCOs had a quick conversation in their native language before he queried Graze. "Okay, we understand. We load, and you shoot eight of the drones quickly. Will four be enough to kill the murderous bastard? Pavel thinks we should send all eight to the breakfast party, actually."

Pete answered him, "We have ten of the big drones—five with armor-piercing, high-explosive warheads similar to the Javelins. The other five have anti-personnel warheads. We will hit the mystery vehicle with anti-armor and the dining tent with two fragmentation warheads. They will detonate thirty feet above the tent and spray a large area with over 2,000 red hot metal shards. We will make blood soup today. Four will be enough for the general. Target #2 is even more important for the counteroffensive to succeed."

"Sounds easy," said Dmytryi. "Push some buttons and watch them die on TV." He laughed and said, "My kind of war."

"The trick will be to stay alive long enough to watch the show," responded Pete in a grave voice.

"So, what about target #3?" asked Pavel.

"Target 3 is a small airport not too far from the village." Pointing to the map, he added a third red dot, about twenty klicks south of their planned firing position. As Graze zoomed in on the image, it was clear that they were looking at an airport. The twelve-hour-old satellite imagery showed at least forty visible Hind-17 and Hind-24 helicopters parked in three main locations. The runway wasn't long enough for heavy cargo planes or fighter jets, but there were several smaller craft visible near a small hangar at the north end of the airport.

Pete told the men, "The plan for #3 is to close from our initial firing position to within five to seven km of the airport. From that vantage, we will launch all 24 of our S300 Tweety Bird drones. Each of the attack drones will be set to detonate on contact, and we will target as many helicopters as we can. Once we launch the Tweeties, we get the hell out of there and escape back to the Ukrainian lines." The men knew from practicing in Poland that the 40 mm fragmentation warheads were highly effective on helicopters and light vehicles.

With that, Graze declared they would move out in ten minutes and head for their firing position. Dmytryi studied his watch for a moment. "We have less than two and one-half hours to travel 40 km and launch the drones. We will need good luck." He squeezed the small gold cross around his neck and closed his eyes, silently mouthing a prayer. "Luck and help from above, I hope."

Before loading into the Dagger, Aleksandr quizzed the general. "Tell me, sir, what was in the bag that you gave the

Russian?”

“Yes, tell us,” echoed the other crew members.

“Two bottles of vodka and a carton of Marlboros. The Russian who cannot be bribed has never been born.” That got everyone chuckling and joking while they cleaned up their camp. Pistol Pete watched in quiet approval of the Ukrainian soldiers. He felt at times as a father or uncle to the young men. He stood twisting the end of his mustache for a full minute, relishing in the pride and fighting off the fear.

While the men stood burning down their last cigarettes, Pete approached the three. “Okay, men, listen up. We got lucky once with a bribe, but soon we will be trading bullets and blood for our passage into the belly of this great beast. Everyone needs to gear up, load up, and check weapons.” Looking at Dmytryi, he added, “That means all your gear. So get your ballistic vest on.”

The three soldiers responded in unison, “Yes, sir!” and quickly took their positions in the Dagger, which lumbered once again east as the first hints of daylight colored the horizon.

They soon discovered that traffic on the road was very congested. There were many heavy tanks and trucks moving to the front lines. They found themselves constantly pulling off the road to give way to the priority traffic. The men knew that the slow pace jeopardized their launch window, so Pete got on the intercom with a proposed solution. “Graze, I know this area. I spent summers here working the fields. I know some side roads and farm tracks that should be clear. The rain has made the ground soft, so there won't be any cargo trucks on those lanes."

Graze agreed to try Pete's country roads tactic, and the driver, Dmytryi, took them north on a dirt road for about two kilometers. In the predawn darkness, Pete managed to find the tractor path he was hoping to find. The ground was very wet, but the tracked BMP easily managed to move ahead along the field's edge.

They eventually transitioned to a gravel road that allowed more speed. That road led directly to the south edge of the ruined village where they planned to launch. The RQ-11 was flying, which allowed Graze to survey the area around the village. He was disappointed to find three groups of Russian soldiers, and vehicles bivouacked near the village. He sent the drone south and soon found a secluded spot along the tree line next to a large sunflower field. They parked the Dagger in a concealed position with an open launch window for the Big Birds. It was 0632 hrs.

The Dagger was equipped with two brackets on each side of the turret which allowed the four-foot-long, 54-pound attack drones to be attached directly to the vehicle. A compressor and air tank in the Dagger provided air pressure to launch the drones. Within ten minutes, the four drones were online and ready for flight. Graze typed in the geolocation for the general's breakfast and at exactly 0700, called out, "All clear! Launching in three . . . two . . . one!" The NCOs watched in silent amazement as the Big Birds popped out of the tubes with a 'whoosh' of air, about five seconds apart. The switchblade wings sprung open, and the silent propeller sent the drones sequentially into the dawning light of day.

Pete called down to them, "Don't just stand there! Get the next group up and ready!" The men unlatched and removed the spent tubes and had four more in place in just a few minutes. Graze sent location information to the guidance units on each drone, and at 0714; they were all on their way to the S-400 Command and Control Center. Once the drones were launched, the NCOs disposed of the empty tubes and got busy on the rear deck of the Dagger. They removed and stowed the lids on the two twelve-pack Tweety launchers and powered up each drone.

As soon as the men were finished, Tariq and Pete switched on their control tablets and ran a system check on the smaller drones. After a minute, Pete reported over the intercom. "Blue unit—all twelve Tweeties are online. Comms are good, built-in test good, battery power all above 95%."

After a moment, Tariq reported the same status for his twelve drones.

Graze acknowledged, "Roger that. "Twenty-four Tweety

Birds ready to leave the nest. Keep them in standby mode for the airport."

At 0721, the first four Big Birds assigned to target #1 began to report "ON STATION." As they did, each drone automatically began circling over the target in wide lazy circles at pre-programmed altitudes of nine to ten thousand feet. Tariq and Pete toggled their screen views to duplicate Graze's. Although Graze was in command of the craft, the men were eager to watch the events unfold.

Graze switched two of the drones to thermal sensor imagery while the other two remained in optical mode. He then carefully locked in the strike points for the four Big Birds. The two anti-armor drones would strike the mystery machine while the two anti-personnel drones would strike the crowd of officers. It would take less than sixty seconds for the deadly birds to dive from ten thousand feet.

They could see a large crowd of officers, staff, and attendants milling around the dining area of the target zone with the mysterious shrouded weapon system parked nearby. At 0720, the status lights for the four drones began to blink green and yellow. The men all understood the Big Birds had fifteen minutes of flight time left. A minute later, the crowd cleared, and five men could be seen approaching the dining tents. Pete was first to exclaim on the intercom, "It's him, Graze! It has to be the Butcher and his security detail. KILL THE DOGS!"

As Graze's finger hovered over the red ATTACK button, his mind raced. Was it really him? Was he about to kill the Butcher of Aleppo? Time seemed to stand still as they all were transfixed by the images before them.

Chapter 11: The Spy

Earlier that fateful morning, General Dvornikov was up at his usual time of 0545. He slipped on his robe and slippers and headed out to the small living room of his mobile living quarters, which consisted of a bedroom with a king bed and wardrobes, a small living area with a TV, and a large bathroom suite with a steam shower.

His quarters were custom-built and heavily armored. He had commissioned its building in 2013, prior to his deployment to Syria, and it was transportable by rail or truck. Whenever the general traveled to a war zone, the trailer was sent ahead of him as part of a small complex of similar units that provided communications, quarters for his security detail, and a well-equipped kitchen.

Dvornikov jokingly referred to his small complex as "The American Express" because he *never left home without it,* which was a tagline in a 1980s TV commercial for American Express Travelers Checks. None of his subordinates understood the joke, but naturally, they all laughed when he said it.

His orderly had brought a thermos of black coffee just minutes earlier, and the general poured a hot cup as he sat on his Ethan Allen sofa. He loved to tell everyone it was a very expensive American sofa that had been manufactured in St

Petersburg. He usually waited a few seconds for his listeners to puzzle over that before telling them, "St Petersburg, *Florida."* Like the American Express reference, very few people actually understood it.

As Dvornikov drank his coffee, he turned on the TV, saying out loud to himself, "Let's see what the *duraks* on CNN have to say." At 0600 hours exactly, there was a single loud knock on the trailer door, and a voice outside announced, "Breakfast, sir!" The general shouted the single word *prikhodit!* from the sofa, and immediately a slender, smartly uniformed private named Nikoly Aslanov entered.

Placing a covered silver tray on the low table in front of Dvornikov, the private asked, "Will there be anything else, sir?"

"Not now. Wait outside with the guard." The young private snapped to attention with a klick of his heels, saluted, and left.

The general lifted the silver cover and was pleased to see and smell the delicious breakfast that had been prepared for him. He took a bite of the thick-sliced Russian black bread flavored with molasses, then he dipped a piece of bread into the buckwheat porridge and took another big satisfying bite. He ate leisurely as some CNN talking head relayed the latest destruction caused by cruise missile attacks on Kiev and Lviv. He laughed out loud and, in a mocking voice, said to no one, "Oh, such a tragedy. Poor Ukrainians. Wait till they see what I will do to these swine!"

The destruction of the Eastern Ukrainian army! This would be the general's crowning achievement. After the pathetic debacle in Kiev, Dvornikov had been summoned to a meeting with President Putin and given command of the Russian Special Operation. Putin reminded the general of his well-earned reputation for brutality and slaughter of civilians in Chechnya and Syria. "Many call you the Butcher of Allepo," Putin had said. "You must now become the Butcher of Ukraine. Turn their cities into dust, General, and do it quickly. On May 9th, I hope to stand in Red Square on Victory Day and celebrate the destruction of the Ukrainian Army.

"Will you stand with me on our great national holiday, or will you be . . . someplace *less pleasant,* should we say?" The consequences of failure were clearly understood by both men. That was just two weeks ago, and now here he was - The Great General Aleksandr Dvornikov - poised on the verge of his greatest success. He smugly thought to himself, "Ah, what a great day!"

The general refilled his coffee and glanced down at the notecards for his speech to be given at 0730. He read and mumbled to himself for a few minutes while finishing breakfast. Just then, he heard his name mentioned by some retired American general on the CNN network—some lazy, stupid, no-name has-been who didn't know his *zhopa* from a hole in the ground. He switched off the television and headed to his bathroom, calling as he did for his orderly.

Private Aslanov was expecting the call, as he did every morning. The general had finished breakfast and was about to retire to his spacious bathroom for the next thirty minutes. Nikoly entered, pushing a cart of fresh linen and cleaning supplies when he was sure that Dvornikov was locked in the bathroom. After cleaning up breakfast, Nikoly switched on the TV in the bedroom and quietly watched CNN while he changed the sheets and made the bed. Satisfied, he retrieved the general's uniform from the closet and carefully laid it out on the bed. Normally Dvornikov just wore simple camouflage attire, but today he had instructed Nikoly to prepare the highly ornate dress uniform, which was plastered with ribbons and medals. After all—this is a very special day.

Nikoly was glad to see the American newsman, Anderson Cooper, broadcasting. The CNN anchor spoke carefully and deliberately, which made a good opportunity to practice his own English. He also thought Cooper to be quite handsome and especially admired his haircut. He vowed to himself that when the war was over, and he was a free man again in Moscow, he would get his hair cut exactly like that. "I'll call it the Cooper Cut," he thought with a smile.

Nikoly was well aware of how easily Dvornikov could

have him executed for even the smallest mistake. The general valued his privacy and was especially disdainful of seeing or speaking to his staff more than necessary, especially conscripts like Private Aslanov. The sound of the shower running was Nikoly's cue to switch off the TV and finish his duties, hastily gathering the cleaning supplies and soiled laundry onto his cart.

Before leaving, Nikoly made one last pass through the rooms, pausing to use a lint roller over the parade uniform and check the shoes for any errant speck of dust. He was pushing the cart out the door when he heard the shower turn off and thought to himself, "No matter how well you shower, nothing can wash away the blood on your soul, and today you will be judged."

Whatever Dvornikov may have assumed or known about his orderly, there were certainly some things that he did not know. The general knew that his orderly was highly recommended by the officer he had previously served in Moscow and that the private was very neat, well-spoken, and attentive. If, however, the entire truth were known, Aslanov and his entire family in Moscow would be dead.

The young private had arrived in Ukraine on April 8th, ten days ahead of the general. He had been dispatched as part of the advance team that set up the general's command post and quarters. After the initial flurry of activity, there was little for the young private to do until Dvornikov's arrival.

The secure area was well behind the front lines, and Nikoly often enjoyed leisurely walks near the rural village nearby. One afternoon, Nikoly was walking and smiling with appreciation for the warm sun on his face and the fragrant apple blossoms nearby.

The uneven wall beside the dirt road dipped to the perfect height to sit, and so he did, basking in the sunshine and feeling good for a few moments. The war seemed so far away as Nikoly closed his eyes and leaned back. That peaceful moment listening to songbirds in the warm sunshine was interrupted when a sound caught his attention. Nikoly opened his eyes to see a small, frail figure shuffling towards him from the village.

Aware of the standing order not to fraternize with the local citizens, Nikoly glanced around nervously while he decided what to do. Before he could make up his mind, however, the decision was made for him. The old woman stopped directly in front of him. He found himself listening to an old lady speaking in fluent and clear Russian. It seemed to Nikoly that the voice did not match the person. It should have been rough and parched, even raspy perhaps, to match her sun-cracked face, not the sweet clear voice that spoke to him.

Nikoly had yet to speak with a Ukrainian since his arrival, and he was keen to make a good impression. Russian culture placed a high value on elders, and it was quite common for a younger person to refer to elderly women or men as grandmother or grandfather, so it was that Nikoly found himself listening politely as the old grandmother addressed him. She spoke quietly at first with her head down, then looked up, staring into Nikoly's eyes with her once piercing blue eyes—now clouded and tired. As she spoke, she reached into the pocket of her peasant dress, pulling out a handful of something and holding it tightly in her arthritic, scarred hand. She asked his name. He told her, "I am Private Nikoly Aslanov from Moscow."

"Aslanov is a beautiful, strong name. Do you know that it means 'son of the lion'? Please take these, my young lion. Take these seeds, but do not eat them."

He automatically opened his hand and watched her slowly pour a handful of sunflower seeds into his palm.

"Thank you, Grandmother, but why not eat them?"

She stared at him with steely eyes. "Please put them in your pocket and leave them there." The puzzled private obliged by dropping the seeds into his jacket pocket. "Good, now when the brave soldiers of Ukraine kill you, and your body is rotting in the rich soil of Ukraine, sunflowers may grow and bring some beauty into the world you are destroying." She turned and left, leaving Aslanov stunned by her words. That was not at all expected. The encounter really upset the young private, and he spent a rather sleepless night mulling over her words.

The next evening the old woman was waiting again near the same spot. Nikoly went to her immediately and pleaded with her. "Why did you say such horrible things to me? Don't you know we are here to save you, Grandmother? We have come to liberate you from the brutal Ukrainian Nazis. Please, Grandmother," he pleaded, "I don't want to die, and we aren't here to destroy Ukraine."

The old woman seemed to soften and smiled. "I'm sorry I spoke so harshly to you. Perhaps you are a man of honor, a man with a heart." She then laughed, "Well, at any rate, you aren't dead yet, so you may as well eat some good bread." At that, she reached into her tattered bag and retrieved a warm, fresh loaf of bread wrapped in a clean cloth.

Nikoly was surprised at her generosity, but when he reached for the bread, she held the loaf from his grasp for a moment. "You remind me of my grandson. He was so bright and kind. This bread is only for you. This is the bread of truth. Learn the truth, and may God have mercy on your soul."

She walked away then, leaving Nikoly to puzzle over her strange words. He called out to ask her what she meant, but she did not turn back. Fearing someone would see them, he decided to leave the area quickly, thinking he might ask her the next time they met, but he never saw the woman again.

The light was just draining from the April sky by the time Nikoly reached his tent. Alone, he sat on his bunk and began to unwrap the heavy loaf. The bread smelled fantastic, and he couldn't wait to take a bite. As he unwrapped it, he noticed that it had been sliced open on the side. He started to break the bread and was surprised to feel something hard inside. Suddenly a plastic bag with a cell phone inside fell to his bunk from the hollow loaf. "What the hell?" Then he remembered her words . . . "the bread of truth."

He immediately shoved the phone under his mattress. The Russian army strictly forbade any enlisted soldier from having a personal cell phone. If he was caught with it, it could mean the firing squad. He quickly powered the device down, fearing it would ring or beep or somehow make its presence known. He spent most of the night debating what to do with the dangerous contraband and finally decided to see what "truths" the old grandmother meant for him to learn.

The next day, Nikoly found a quiet spot in a nearby orchard to examine the gift. He was surprised to see that it had a sim card, two signal bars, and unlimited data. Over the next few days, Nikoly used the phone to watch many of the western news reports about the so-called Russian Special Operation. From the few glimpses he had gotten from the general's TV, he knew that the official Russian version of events in Ukraine was not entirely true, but he had no idea of the depth of the deception. The whole thing was a giant lie. His country wasn't "liberating" the poor people of

Ukraine from ruthless Nazis, as the Russian version was told. Far from it, in fact.

Nikoly also used the phone to call his family in Moscow and was shocked to learn that his sister and brother-in-law had been arrested for war protests there. His parents called his sister a traitor and fool. He tried to tell them about the slaughter of civilians in Bucha, bombed kindergartens, and destroyed cities, but they were hopelessly brainwashed by Russian state TV. His father was angry with Nikoly, demanding, "Where did you learn such lies? How can you call yourself a Russian soldier and talk such traitorous nonsense?" He was deeply saddened that his own parents believed their son had lost his mind—or worse. It would be the last time he spoke with his family.

Nearly a week passed without encountering any other locals on his daily walks until one day, an elderly man was waiting very near the spot where he had spoken with the old lady. Nikoly felt nervous and ashamed as he approached the old man, so much so that he nearly turned and fled. Just then, the man smiled and asked, "Do you know the truth now, Nikoly?"

Aslanov began shaking and burst into tears in front of the man. Practically falling to his knees, he cried out, "Yes! My God, yes! I am so sorry and so ashamed, but what can I do, Grandfather?"

The old man patted him gently on the shoulder. "Well,

I'm glad you asked that question. If you are serious, there is much you can do."

Nikoly wiped away the tears on his cheek. "What can I do, Grandfather? I am just a simple private."

The old man then gently placed both hands on Nikoly's shoulders and whispered, "Help us stop this madness. You know more than you realize, my son."

That was the day the Ukrainian resistance gained their most important spy.

Private Aslanov continued to take his walks when off-duty and secretly exchanged notes with the Ukrainian resistance. There was a low stone wall, partially hidden in the woods near his route. It was common for Russian soldiers in the area to relieve themselves against the wall, so it was that Nikoly often did the same. Once a day, he would hide a small piece of paper with information behind a certain rock. The notes covered personnel, equipment, vehicles, locations of troops, and, of course, any information on General Dvornikov since his arrival on April 18th. Nikoly's Ukrainian counterparts also left notes for him in the same location, asking very specifically about the big breakfast party planned for Monday, April 25th.

On Sunday evening, April 24th, Aslanov dropped his note as usual and headed back towards camp. As he was passing the small orchard, he was surprised to encounter his Ukrainian recruiter just off the roadway. The old man motioned for the Russian private to come near, and he spoke in a low, conspiratorial tone. "I see you are still alive, Nikoly. That's good." He then grasped the private's face gently and turned it from side to side. "You look like you are getting ill—perhaps just a cold. You should stay in bed tomorrow morning for your health."

Aslanov replied with a puzzled smile, "I feel fine, Grandfather."

"Please, I should not say this to you, but you must listen to me. Stay away from the general's breakfast party." With that, the man walked away at a brisk pace. Nikoly understood the warning well enough. Surely there would be some sort of attack in the morning, but he feared his absence might raise suspicions and possibly disrupt the deadly plans he had helped to make. So Nikoly got up and performed his duties as usual, serving coffee and laying out Dvornikov's dress uniform. Though he did not know exactly what would happen at 0730, he was sure something very bad was planned for the Butcher and two hundred of his battalion commanders and staff.

Having completed his morning duties, the nervous private waited outside near the door until he was dismissed by the general's four-man personal security detail. At exactly 0725, Dvornikov came outside to begin the two-hundred-meter walk to the gathering, flanked by the heavily armed guards.

As soon as they started away, Nikoly turned and moved at a fast pace in the opposite direction. A minute later, he was crouched behind a small building with his heart pounding fiercely in his chest. Noting the time on his watch as 0731, he started to wonder if the old man had been wrong or if the attack had been postponed, when four loud explosions in rapid succession came from the direction of the party. He waited a full minute and then quickly moved towards the rally.

Within a few steps, he began to hear the agonized screaming of wounded and dying men. He could also see the flames from a burning vehicle as heavy smoke filled the morning air. He cautiously moved closer as dozens of walking and running wounded men swept past him, bloodied and terrified. Suddenly Nikoly came face to face with General Dvornikov and a severely wounded member of his security detail.

The general was white as a sheet and trembling, his uniform dirty and blood-stained. The terrified general grabbed Aslanov by the shoulders, demanding to know where the helicopters were. The private knew that many of the high-ranking guests had arrived by helicopters, which were parked in a nearby field. Nikoly led the men through a small hedge to find at least six of them.

The general limped up to the nearest MI-8, where two pilots were waiting. They saluted in surprise when they realized who he was. Dvornikov asked if the craft was ready to make the short flight to the airport. Both officers replied, "Yes, sir!" The general climbed aboard and turned to see his security guard collapse a few feet from the door. As Nikoly stopped to help the man up, Dvornikov shouted, "Leave the fool and get inside *now*!" Aslanov looked down at the dying man as if to apologize just as the stricken soldier breathed his last, and the light flew from his eyes. He closed the dead man's eyes and boarded the craft as the wheels began to leave the ground.

The pilots were ordered to contact the airport and have the general's private airplane ready to leave right away, which of course, they did. Fifteen minutes later, the helicopter touched down fifty yards from the sleek twin-engine aircraft. General Dvornikov, followed by Aslanov, immediately approached the plane to find a young Russian captain nervously waiting in his multi-zippered Nomex flight suit.

By this time, the Ukrainian counter-offensive had already begun along the entire Russian frontlines, and fiery explosions could be seen and heard in every direction as dawn broke the eastern sky. The frightened pilot saluted and started to ask what was happening when a booming explosion nearby interrupted his question, causing all three men to drop to the ground.

When the men got to their feet again, Divornikov was

visibly shaken and demanded they take off immediately, climbing the stairs into the cabin as he spoke. The captain quickly pulled the wheel chocks and several red-tagged "Remove Before Flight" devices from the aircraft and stowed them. He stood waiting on the tarmac near the open door for about a minute when the general appeared and barked, "What are you waiting for? Let's go NOW!

"Sir, your plane is fueled and ready for flight. I am just waiting for the copilot to arrive."

"You can fly it alone! Start the engines and take off immediately!"

"Yes, sir! What is our destination, sir?"

"Kubinka Air Base, Moscow. Fly as fast as possible and stay below the radar!"

The pilot climbed through the open door and secured it before taking his place at the controls in the left seat. Within a few seconds, the starboard engine was started, and the aircraft began to taxi as the port engine spun into life. Five minutes later, the graceful AN-26 was off the ground and turning due north to Moscow. While the aircraft gained altitude, the shaken Dvornikov settled into his opulent, mahogany-trimmed VIP lounge in the aft, pouring a tall glass of vodka to settle his nerves. Aslanov sat in the forward section in one of the twelve seats there, behind the pilot.

After a few minutes, Dvornikov called his orderly back

to him and ordered the private to locate a medical kit. The general had several cuts on his neck and shoulder from shrapnel. Aslanov moved forward again and leaned into the cockpit slightly to ask about the kit.

The pilot pulled his right headset off and partially turned. "What do you want?" Aslanov asked if there was a medical kit on board. Flying without a copilot, the captain was busy with the controls and radios and annoyed by the interruption. "First overhead bin behind me." The bin popped open, and sure enough, there was a large medical kit inside.

Private Aslanov could see through the pilot's windscreen that they were flying very fast at a low altitude. After delivering the medical kit to the general, Nikoly returned to take the first seat on the starboard side. From there, he could see the pilot and had a clear view out the windscreen as well, mesmerized by what he saw. It felt like they were sailing over a golden sea as the endless wheat fields flashed under them. Aslanov had never been in an aircraft, and he sat transfixed by the scene in front of him for a few moments. Suddenly, bellowing from the aft interrupted his thoughts. "Get back here, you *durak*!"

The private unbuckled his seat belt and stooped in the aisle, glancing to the rear where the fat pig sat, motioning for him. Aslanov was stunned when he looked forward through the windscreen. The aircraft was approaching Kharkiv, where the beautiful golden fields of wheat had become a nightmare. He was stunned by the destruction he witnessed. The vast city was laid bare and dotted with smoking ruins and fires. When the general shouted again, the pilot turned and warned Nikoly to sit down or go to the rear.

Private Nikoly Aslanov's head was spinning. The fast-moving events and immense destruction had shocked him to his very core. He stood in the aisle, frozen in thought for a moment, then looked again at the burning city below them and then back at the general, then at the pilot. He knew at that moment he would never see his mother and father again. He knew he would not see Moscow again or the lover who waited there for his return. He would not celebrate the end of this war nor ever get that cool Cooper haircut that he had imagined.

When the general shouted again from the rear, Nikoly made the decision that he knew he must. He threw his body over the right shoulder of the pilot, who had only time to let out a short, terrified scream. The man was helpless to do anything as the private's full body weight fell on the yoke, pitching the craft instantly down into a fireball seconds later.

Chapter 12: Attack

Graze was just about to press the flashing red ATTACK button on his console when gunshots and shouts erupted around the Dagger. From inside his compartment, he heard shouts in Russian and Ukrainian, and the gunfire stopped as suddenly as it had started. Graze sat in stunned silence for a few moments while he unholstered his sidearm, trying to imagine what was going on outside. He heard more talking in Ukrainian and what sounded like children.

Then Pete's voice could be heard speaking cautiously in English. "Hello, Graze. We have a certain situation here. Could you very slowly peek out and take a look?" Graze did as requested and was surprised to find that a small farm wagon pulled by an emaciated donkey had gotten within about twenty yards of their position. The Dagger crew had been preoccupied and didn't see the wagon approach until the occupants opened fire on them. Graze now took stock of their attackers—six Ukrainian boys who looked to be about ages nine to twelve.

A red-headed youth who was apparently the leader was standing in the wagon holding a double-barrel shotgun. The other boys were armed, as it were, with a couple of revolvers, knives, axes, and yes, one actually held a pitchfork. The attack had taken the Dagger crew completely unawares, but within seconds Pavel and Dmytryi had drawn their sidearms and taken defensive positions.

In that split second, Smirnov leapt from the tank and landed surprisingly cat-like on the ground between the boys and the tank. He held up his hands as if to surrender while the redhead fumbled to reload his gun. Pete tossed his own pearl-handled pistol to the ground and motioned his men to lower their weapons. Speaking in Ukrainian, he said to the boys, "My name is General Peotr Smirnov, Commander of the Ukrainian Territorial Defence Forces of the Ground Forces Command. Please lower your weapons, and I will explain."

The red-haired boy finished dropping two shells into the breach of the shotgun and snapped it closed but did not raise it to fire. "Liar! You speak Ukrainian, but we can plainly see that you are Russian soldiers. We can see the big letter Z on your tank!" Before Pete could answer, Pavel stepped clear of the Dagger and began to sing softly, then louder, as the other NCOs joined him in singing the Ukrainian National Anthem. Confusion flashed across the faces of the young boys, and it quickly turned to smiles and then cheers.

When the song finished, Pete motioned the boys down from their battle wagon, and the six children gathered in a small semi-circle in front of him. Pete let out a great sigh of relief and turned to Graze, who was still watching from his hatch on the Dagger. "All good here, Graze. Do your job now."

"Yes, sir. Is anyone hurt?"

Pete glanced over at the NCOs, who shook their heads, indicating no injuries. Looking at his own bloody left sleeve, he replied, "Nothing serious. Get to work; I got this."

Several pellets from the shotgun blast had bloodied his arm, but Pete knew it was not serious. While Graze and the rest of the crew were busy, Pete and Aleksandr attended to their attackers. Alex grabbed some rations and water from the Dagger and distributed them while Pete had the boys introduce themselves. The leader was named Felix, and he was thirteen. The other five, ages nine to eleven, were Yakiv, Oleg, Stepan, Pylyp, and Vanko. All the boys were wearing ragged, filthy clothes and ate and drank what they were offered as if they hadn't eaten in days.

The group continued in Ukrainian as Felix explained that their village had been destroyed, and they were alone and tired of hiding. They decided to fight and called themselves the *Pocomaxa,* Ukrainian for wolverine. Pete gave them a curious look with a turned-up eyebrow when he heard that.

Felix seemed surprised that the general did not understand. "You know, like the American movie *Red Dawn.* We are the Wolverines, though without Patrick Swayze, of course."

Pete was still not following, but Alex understood the reference. "Yes, yes, wolverines. I like it!" To the general, he said, "It's an old American fiction movie about a group of boys who fight Russians that invade the United States."

"And this Patrick Swayze?" inquired Pete.

"He is a famous American movie star," Felix answered. "In our home, we had many American movies on DVD, but why are you driving a Russian tank and wearing Russian uniforms, General?" Pete held up a finger and listened for a few seconds on his earbud as Graze announced the drone attack on the breakfast party would begin in three minutes. This was Pete's cue to finish up with the boys and get ready to move out for the airport.

"Well, you see, we are on a secret mission to attack our enemies, so we are pretending to be Russians. We have much work to do, so now you must leave us." While the boys returned to the wagon, Pete quickly retrieved an AK-47, two extra mags, and a frag grenade from the Dagger. Handing the weapons to Felix, Pete asked if he knew how to use them.

"I know how to use the AK-47, and the grenade is simple: pull the pin, count to five, and throw it, right?"

"Count to three to be safe, ok?" Then he stood at attention and issued an order in his most official-sounding voice: "I, General Peotr Smirnov, now give this order to the Wolverine unit of the Eastern Ukrainian Ground Forces. You are to immediately move to a safe place and await further orders. Do NOT attack any Russians, but defend yourselves with all your power if you are found. Move out!"

As the boys climbed back in the wagon, Pete pulled Felix aside and took a softer familial tone with the boy. "You are all brave young men of Ukraine, but your job, Felix, is now to protect these boys under your command." Pointing to his bloody sleeve, Pete chuckled as he said, "One day, when you are an old man, you will tell your grandsons of 'The Day of the Dagger'—the day you shot the great General Smirnov."

Felix flushed red and started to apologize, but Pete cut him off. "Don't worry, son. Of all the times I have been shot, this is the least and most memorable of wounds. Get moving now, and stay hidden and safe."

"Yes, sir, General. I'm sorry I shot you."

"Don't worry about me, but I have one last question for you, Felix. You came from the south. Did you see any Russian checkpoints between here and the airport?"

"We did see one at least, about two kilometers south from here. One tank and other vehicles with about twenty men."

"Thank you, Felix. Now go in the opposite direction, and go with God."

As the Wolverines started off, Pete returned to his position in the turret while Tariq and the other men climbed onto the Dagger to watch the attacks. The four Big Birds had been circling at ten thousand feet before they began their dives at 125 mph. The drones targeting the canopies detonated first over the crowd of officers, and of course, the video from them instantly blanked out. The two anti-armor Big Birds were just seconds behind the first two, and the men's eyes were glued to the monitors as they saw the general fall to the ground and then begin to crawl away from the area. The last two drones went blank upon impact, and it was not immediately clear if the general had escaped or not.

There was no time to worry about that, however. Graze double-checked the target lock for the drones circling the Russian S-400 control center and launched the attack on the secondary target. Sixty seconds later, those images also went dark. The attacks were over—though to what effect was uncertain at that point. The men loaded the last two Big Birds onto the turret, and the Dagger growled to life with a billow of smoke and headed toward the airport at 0737. Graze was curious about the encounter with the Ukrainian boys, and Pete explained that he had given the boys some weapons and rations and sent them north to be safe. Pavel jumped in and said, "Sir, they were headed south when I last saw them."

The farm track soon became too muddy to traverse, so Pete reluctantly ordered Alex to maneuver onto the blacktop road leading to the airport. On the intercom, Pete informed the crew that the Wolverines had spotted a checkpoint nearby. There was no other traffic, so they moved cautiously and prepared to talk their way through. Pete spotted the checkpoint with binoculars from about one klick out, and sure enough, there was a tank and a BTR blocking the road. He ordered a halt to prepare for their ruse when a loud explosion was seen and heard from the checkpoint, followed by automatic weapons fire.

"What the hell?" Pete uttered. "Okay, let's go. This may be easier than we hoped." A few minutes later, the Dagger pulled up and stopped about thirty yards from a scene of chaos. The T-80 tank was burning, and several dead Russian soldiers were on the ground near the tank.

A Russian lieutenant ran up to the Dagger with his hand held up, shouting excitedly. "Do you have any first aid supplies, Major?" We have several wounded men here!"

"What the hell happened, Lieutenant?"

The lieutenant pointed to a small farm wagon on the shoulder near the burning tank. Pete instantly recognized the wagon, though it was shot to pieces, and the donkey lay bleeding and bawling on the ground.

"These little bastards stopped and offered to trade vegetables and bread for rations. The red-haired boy climbed on the tank with a bag of food but dropped a grenade down the hatch instead. Then the others opened fire with shotguns and automatic weapons. We killed them all, but we lost six men, and four are wounded. I shot the red-haired leader myself when he jumped from the tank."

The blood was boiling in Pete's face as he surveyed the

scene. Anger and sadness filled his being in a way he had never felt before, as he counted the six dead boys sprawled on the wagon and on the road. "Just give me a moment to explain to my crew, Lieutenant."

Pete slumped into the turret, keyed the intercom, and through gritted teeth, with a shaking voice, spoke to the crew. "There is a BTR at ten o'clock at thirty meters with six soldiers near the vehicle and nine or ten more at two o'clock. Tariq, when I open fire, take out the BTR with the cannon and sweep from left to right with the .762. Pavel, Alex—out the back with grenades and AKs. Kill everything that moves. The boys are all dead. Now it is our turn."

As he stood up in the hatch, Pete drew his Colt but held it out of sight from the Russians. "The red-haired boy, the one you killed—his name was Felix."

The lieutenant stood, opened-mouthed. "Felix? How do you kno—?" The loud report of the Colt 45 cut off his question as the back of the man's head disintegrated. The Dagger crew instantly sprung into action. Tariq blew the BTR to pieces with the cannon at point-blank range, then continued with the machine gun as he rotated the turret a full 90 degrees. Dmytryi sprung from the driver's hatch, lobbing a grenade and spraying lead from his AK-74. Pavel and Alex went out the back doing the same. Nine seconds later, the fight was over as every Russian at the checkpoint lay dead.

The Dagger crew took a few tear-soaked minutes to lay

each of the dead boys in the wagon, with their weapons across their tiny chests. There was no time for prayers or burials; instead, the six hardened soldiers stood at attention and saluted the heroism of the Wolverines. Pete's voice wavered as he spoke. "Someday, they may call us heroes, men, but we are soldiers. These innocent children are the real heroes. Let's move out. There are more Russians waiting to die."

The crew reloaded their weapons and clamored back into the Dagger while Pavel was busy beside the T-80 with a rag dipped in Russian blood. He hopped in the rear troop door as the Dagger rumbled into life and started away from the carnage towards the airport. Their heavy hearts would not allow words for several minutes, many saying silent prayers for the brave children. Later that morning, a Russian patrol would come upon the checkpoint and wonder at the Ukrainian word sprawled on the tank fender: *Росомаха.*

Pete, once again, was the only crew member visible, playing the role of an old Russian major. The intercom was deadly silent inside the Dagger, except for enemy radio chatter being keenly monitored by the four Ukrainians on board. Pete was the first to speak. "Men, we are all sad about the Wolverines, but let's clear our minds and keep a close lookout for nosey Russians. We are still twenty klicks from the airport and can't risk flying the Raven yet, so we don't have our 'eye in the sky.'"

The Dagger made good time towards the airport, without further incident, passing through two more checkpoints easily with a wave and smile from Pete. When they were approximately six kilometers from the airport, Pete ordered the vehicle off the main road to follow a tree line down the edge of a vast wheat field. Everything was set for their final assault on the Russians.

Tariq and Pete launched all 24 of the Tweety Birds, and the silent killers climbed towards the airport, soon reaching the pre-planned altitude of 5,000 feet. Graze noted the time was 0815 and thought to himself that with luck, they would be back in Ukrainian territory by lunch, as Mark had predicted. The NCOs launched the RQ-11 for Pete to survey their escape route. Everything was going to plan, which made Graze nervous because he knew that no plan survived for long in combat. The RQ-11 Raven took flight and began to slowly climb out to the west when, sure enough, the plan *and* the drone disintegrated in mid-flight.

A pair of Russian BTRs and a T-72 tank burst onto the field on their right and cut down the drone with heavy machine gun fire. Having shot down the drone, the Russians immediately turned their attention to the Dagger. A shell from the tank exploded very near them just as Aleksandr and Pavel clamored back inside through the rear doors. Pete yelled into the intercom, "GO! FORWARD NOW!" Dymytryi flipped on the turbo, and the Dagger lurched forward at full speed across the field, billowing a smoke screen. They could outrun the Russian tank but not the 125 mm cannon on the T-72. The tank was firing at maximum rate, and high explosive shells were detonating on all sides of the speeding Dagger. Graze launched one of the remaining Big Birds from its turret mount to take out the tank and ordered Pete to redirect four Tweeties to attack the BTRs. Tariq was doing his best to bring the 30 mm autocannon to bear on the Russians as their vehicle bounced at nearly seventy kph through the field.

They knew they had very little time before the Russian cannons found their marks. Pete was working feverishly in the turret of the bouncing BMP to lock the four Tweeties onto the speeding BTRs. He managed to guide three of the four drones onto the turrets of the eight-wheeled armored vehicles. He immediately popped the commander's hatch to verify the kills, just in time to see one of BTRs careen wildly to the left and roll over several times. The second BTR had been stopped, and thick smoke and flames could be seen spewing from the front as its crew evacuated. Pete ducked back inside the relative safety of the Dagger just as a round from the T-72 glanced off the turret, igniting the reactive armor as it did. With a pounding heart and ringing ears, Pete keyed the intercom. "Graze, do you have that T-72? We are running out of time!"

The Big Birds had a safety feature that could not be

overridden: The attack drone would not arm until it reached a minimum altitude of one thousand feet. Graze was nervously watching the tank through the sensors while flying the drone at full power to reach the required altitude. Just then, Dmytryi shouted on the intercom, "GUYS! We are coming to the end of this field, and there is a high chain-link fence! What should I do?" Without hesitation, Pete ordered him to smash through it and keep going at full speed. The crew immediately braced for impact, but there was none as the fourteen-ton BMP cut through the fence like a hot knife through butter. Just as they burst through the fence, Graze pushed the attack button on the control pad, and fifteen seconds later, the drone scored a direct hit on the T-72, which exploded with devastating force.

They suddenly found themselves hurtling down a taxiway with the runway on the right and a long line of hangers filled with and surrounded by Russian helicopters on their left. The twenty remaining attack drones circling overhead were dispatched in short order and rained death and chaos down on a long line of helicopters.

As the Dagger sped down the taxiway, Tariq traversed the turret left and unleashed withering fire from the 30 mm autocannon and coaxial 7.62 machine gun. The open hangars and dozens of helicopters and service vehicles were sitting ducks lined up just a hundred yards from the Dagger. The Russians were caught by complete surprise amid the exploding inferno around them. Few even saw the Dagger, let alone return fire on the speeding vehicle. In less than a minute, the attack was over, and the Dagger slowed and stopped past the last hangar.

Hidden behind a small building, the NCOs quickly loaded the last two Tweeties in the one undamaged launch box while Pete did a quick damage check of the vehicle. The firefight with the Russians outside the airport had taken out the antennas and the turret-mounted anti-tank weapon. Graze confirmed that radio and satellite communications were inoperable. The crew would have to rely on the airborne radar system and the one remaining RQ-11 drone to get home.

Graze consulted his maps while the NCOs launched the surveillance drone, which thankfully climbed unmolested westward. A minute later, the idling Dagger was buttoned up and ready for the escape back to Ukrainian-controlled territory. Graze keyed the intercom to brief the crew on their situation. "Men, we have accomplished everything we came here to do today except the last important part, which is to get out of here alive. We are about forty klicks deep inside Russian territory, and then we have another fifty to the Ukrainian lines. We have just enough fuel, one Big Bird, two Tweeties, and a Stinger missile, plus small arms. Tariq, how much ammo do you have left?"

"Five hundred rounds on the 7.62 and about 150 rounds

of 30 mm. The cannon barrel got extremely hot and is pretty much shot, so I wouldn't count on the 150 rounds."

Pete studied the terrain as the Raven flew to the west and within a minute, decided that they would exit the same way they arrived—by smashing through the perimeter fence to access a farm road nearby. Speaking to the driver, he said, "Okay, nice and easy Dmytryi. Head across the runway at 30 kph and aim for the fence just to the left of the big willow tree."

Two minutes later, Dmytryi sped up and burst through the light fencing. No one seemed to have noticed a solitary Russian BMP in the confusion at the airport. The crew breathed a collective sigh of relief as they embraced the real possibility of escape.

The crew of the Dagger was unaware of the lone Hind attack helicopter that had, in fact, seen them. The MI-24 had left at sunrise to patrol the area south near Mariupol and was returning to base. Colonel Boruff, at the controls, was a seasoned veteran of many combat operations, but he and the gunner in the front cockpit were both stunned to see the base in ruins, with fuel trucks and helicopters burning everywhere they looked. They hovered just outside the base, taking in the destruction, when the gunner pointed out a BMP crashing through the fence and heading west. The pilot sneered, "Run, you coward," thinking it was a Russian vehicle fleeing the carnage.

The returning Hind was critically low on fuel and completely out of ordinance, so the pilot hover-taxied through the mayhem toward a maintenance hangar that had been spared. They saw several helicopters and men inside through the open doors and settled their own helicopter on the tarmac in front of the building. As the engines wound down on the big machine, the pilot and gunner climbed out to learn what had happened.

Spotting another pilot nearby, Colonel Boruff and his gunner ran to question the man, who was kneeling next to an obviously lifeless body. The young lieutenant was clearly in shock and did not respond until Boruff's gunner shook him by the shoulders. "Speak, man! What happened here?"

The man did not get up but turned his head slowly and looked up at the colonel through glazed eyes. His voice shook as he spoke. "I saw the bastards. My gunner and I were walking toward our Hind for a mission when a series of explosions began destroying everything in sight. We were just a few yards away when the nose of our helicopter exploded. A large piece of shrapnel killed my gunner, but I fell to the ground unhurt."

The shaken lieutenant turned again to his friend on the ground and continued. "That's when I saw a single BMP racing along the flightline strafing everything with its cannon. The vehicle passed quickly, but I could see it had Russian markings, and I saw a Russian officer clearly from the waist up above the turret, firing a pistol and laughing like a maniac. Another helicopter exploded near me then, and when I looked up again, the BMP was gone."

Colonel Boruff put two and two together and realized the vehicle he had seen escaping was involved in the attack. His mind raced as he wondered how one BMP could do all this damage. Was it possible?

He found a maintenance officer in the hangar and ordered his Hind to be refueled and rearmed immediately. The lieutenant hurriedly inspected the craft and began barking commands to his maintenance troops. Colonel Boruff asked about the status of the other helicopters in the hangar and was told there was one serviceable Hind that needed fuel and armaments loaded. Boruff ordered the man to have both aircraft ready to fight with all possible haste.

"Yes, Sir. We will do as you order, but it may be difficult to work quickly in this situation." The lieutenant offered the two pilots to wait in his office and had food and water brought to them. After about twenty minutes the maintenance lieutenant returned to the office with the second helicopeter crew and an update.

While the helicopters were being serviced, the four airmen ate and listened to the radio chatter. They were shocked to hear the reports. The S-400 radar net was disabled, and Ukrainian jets and Turkish drones were destroying the mobile launchers and attacking fuel and ammunition depots along the entire Russian front lines—from Donetsk all the way to Mariupol in the south, a distance of nearly 400 km. They listened in stunned silence to reports of naval vessels in the Black Sea being struck by torpedoes and Neptune missiles. The Russian naval base in Sevastopol had also been heavily damaged.

One of the pilots spoke up at that news. "My God, they have destroyed Sevastopol!" They all knew that since 2014 the Russian navy had expanded the naval base, and it was crucial to the Russian invasion of Ukraine. The base served as a port for Russian military operations as well as logistics resupply of the Russian armies in the south.

The colonel tried desperately to get new orders and to report the suspicious BMP they had seen but to no avail. The reports were that General Dvornikov and many senior officers had been killed earlier that morning. It all seemed too impossible. That's when Colonel Boruff decided to take matters into his own hands. He was getting impatient to begin the hunt when the maintenance officer entered to announce that the helicopters were ready for flight.

The four men grabbed their helmets and scrambled out to the tarmac just as the last fuel truck was pulling away. They climbed into the cockpits of the massive gunships and started their engines. Boruff decided they would head west and try to locate the imposters who had played a part in this devastation.

His own aircraft was an older model armed with a 12.7 mm chain gun and two rocket pods. The wing-mounted rocket pods each held 16 of the 55 mm S-5M rockets. Colonel Boruff was disappointed that the more powerful S-5U anti-armor rockets were not available. He knew from long experience that the S-5M was completely ineffective beyond one kilometer due to the tendency of the rockets to spread out. Russian aviators referred to them as the Tulips because of this. He would need to get close to use the Tulips on the armored BMP.

The second MI-24 helicopter had the same 12.7 mm chin turret augmented by two UPK-23-gun pods. The chin guns would have limited effectiveness against the armored BMP, but he was pleased to see the 23 mm twin-barrel gun pods on the other craft. The crews strapped in and hastily checked the systems as the twin 2,200 HP engines spun into life. They were airborne at 1045 hours.

The colonel calculated that their prey had a two-hour head start, but the MI-24 Hind helicopters were extremely fast, with a top speed of 350 kph. The two-ship formation quickly reached top speed, and he was determined and confident that they would catch and destroy the saboteurs.

The pair of killer helicopters monitored Russian radio traffic and repeatedly transmitted a request for any sighting of their prey. Nearing the Russian front lines, they were contacted with the information they sought. Thirty minutes earlier, a BMP had burst through their checkpoint, destroying a T-72 and a BMP-3. The vehicle had run the checkpoint and was being pursued by two BTR-80s as it sped west on Route 31. Colonel Boruff cinched his harness tighter and smiled to himself. He keyed the microphone and ordered the second ship to follow in trail position at a distance of one kilometer.

Chapter 13: Escape

Forty-five minutes earlier, the Dagger made a pit stop under the shelter of a ruined barn just four kilometers from the last Russian checkpoint blocking escape. As soon as the BMP shut down, the six men hopped out to stretch, hydrate and check out their equipment.

Graze and Pete conferred together for a few minutes, and then Pete climbed up on the turret while Graze called the men together near the open rear doors of the Dagger to brief them. "Look, a couple klicks down this road, around the bend, is the last Russian checkpoint between us and freedom. Without radios, we have to assume that the entire Russian army is looking for us. So, there will be no talking our way past this one. We are gonna hit 'em hard and fast and just keep going. There is one T-72 tank, a BMP-3, two of the fast, newer BTR-80s, plus about a hundred men. The road itself is only blocked by barbed wire. The plan is that we launch our last remaining Big Bird and move to a point about one kilometer from the Russians, hidden by the turn of the road. We will charge through their position as soon as the Big Bird explodes on the tank."

Graze continued with individual instructions for the NCOs.

"Dmytryi, when I say go, turn on the smoke screen and

the turbo and move at full speed right through the intersection and just keep going.”

“Got it.”

“Pavel and Alex, pop the rear hatches and spray everything with your AKs. As soon as we are clear, get the four mines ready to go in case the BTRs give chase. Also, get the Stinger missile out and handy.

“Tariq, you will open fire on the BTRs, but wait until the Big Bird hits.”

“Roger that. Let’s hope the cannon is up to the job.”

While the men were talking, Pete was busy on top of the turret. He had removed the Russian unit banner from the mast and replaced it with a 3’x5’ Ukrainian flag. He called down to the group, “I say it is time to show the true colors of our great land!”

They all shouted their approval and removed their Russian uniform jackets. Pavel took the extra measure to throw his coat down and grind it with his boot. They all had a last drink or bite to eat, checked their ammo, and took up their positions in the Dagger. Dmytryi slowly rolled down the road while Graze launched the last Big Bird. About one klick from the Russians, Pete got on the intercom. “Okay, men, it's now or never. Graze, is the Big Bird in position?”

Graze had the drone circling above the Russians at 5,000 feet, locked onto the T-72. “Yes, sir. Starting attack now.

Dmytryi, get ready . . . 5 . . . 4 . . . 3 . . 2 . . . 1 . . . GO!"

The surprised Russians had not opened fire or even seen the BMP charging towards them when the T-72 erupted in flames with an ear-splitting explosion. Just seconds later, the Dagger came smashing through the barricade at high speed with guns blazing.

A commander of one of the BTRs poked his head out just in time to get a glimpse of the attackers. He could scarcely believe his eyes. The vehicle he saw was billowing smoke and had a large blue and yellow flag flying from the turret. A secondary explosion from the burning tank made him duck back inside. When the smoke was beginning to clear, he looked out again to see the tank and the BMP destroyed and dozens of dead or wounded soldiers scattered about. The stunned vehicle commander ordered the second BTR to follow him, and he began pursuit. He knew that the BTR-80s were capable of 85 kph on blacktop which should allow them to overtake the BMP in less than ten minutes.

The Dagger fled along the paved road at top speed, burning precious fuel in turbo mode. Graze monitored the radar system for enemy aircraft while Pete and Tariq watched the road to their rear for pursuing Russians. After ten minutes, Tariq reported the ominous news that he had spotted a vehicle on the road behind them and it was closing on them. Pete studied his sighting system and confirmed that the two BTRs from the checkpoint were in pursuit.

The general keyed the intercom ordering the NCOs to prepare to release all four land mines. A few moments later, he spotted a narrow bridge ahead, arching over a stream. The perfect spot to set a trap, he thought. "As soon as we cross the bridge ahead, release all four mines quickly. Let's hope they will be hidden from our Russian friends by the rise of the bridge." Just as the Dagger crossed the bridge, Pete yelled, "NOW!"

Dmytryi transitioned from one side of the road to the other as the four mines skidded out randomly on the pavement. The Dagger picked up speed again, with all eyes on the bridge behind them. Suddenly the lead BTR could be seen on the bridge, and seconds later, it erupted in a violent fireball, having struck one of the mines. The second BTR had seen enough and stopped on the bridge to aid their injured comrades.

Several men burst into cheers, but the crew's celebration was short-lived as the radar system then sounded on the intercom with an ominous warning: "AIRCRAFT DETECTED!" Graze studied the display and soon identified two aircraft eighteen kilometers due east of the Dagger, traveling at 350 kph at an altitude of 200 meters. "Two Hinds are about three minutes behind us and closing fast. We are no match for the helicopters in the open countryside. Any ideas?"

A long five seconds passed as the men considered their

options. Pete was the first to respond. "Graze, didn't Sam say that it was theoretically possible to shoot down a helicopter with a Tweety Bird if the target was flying directly at them at low altitude?"

"Yes! Yes, he did!" Graze answered. "And we have nothing left to lose at this point! Power up the last two Tweeties and send them east, Pete." Twenty seconds later, the birds popped out of their launch boxes and were headed back in the direction they had come, locked onto the two helicopters.

The drones were within ten seconds of impact when the lead helicopter turned sharply and began a long sweeping turn that would bring it to bear on the Dagger from the north. The small drone attempted to follow but could not overtake the helicopter. The second Hind maintained its heading directly toward the Dagger and was soon visible to the crew in the turret, less than two kilometers away. The gunner in the Hind opened fire, and the tracer rounds began whizzing bright red death, getting ever closer to the Dagger. Invisible to everyone was the Tweety Bird on a collision course with a combined closing velocity of nearly 500 kph.

The gunner managed to squeeze off a few more rounds before the Tweety impacted the nose of the helicopter. The explosive force of the warhead shredded the entire forward section of the Hind, instantly killing both crewmembers and pitching the craft steeply into the ground. Colonel Boruff turned his head in time to see the massive fireball, and cursed aloud before continuing his attack on the BMP from the north.

The BMP was approaching another bridge spanning a dirt road beneath it and was attempting to seek cover while billowing a smoke screen. Colonel Boruff gave the order to open fire with the chin gun and the starboard rocket pod. The sixteen rockets launched in rapid sequence, causing the helicopter to yaw to starboard, spoiling the gunner's aim. Boruff could see that many of the rockets exploded on the bridge and behind the BMP, but he was certain several had found their mark. Boruff continued forward over the bridge, intending to turn and finish them off from the south.

The men inside the severely damaged Dagger were reeling from the attack. Pete's right arm and shoulder were a mess of blood and torn clothing, but he remained conscious. As the vehicle came to a stop under the bridge, Tariq helped the Ukrainian general apply a tourniquet to stem the blood loss. Two of the rockets had exploded on the Dagger just forward of the driver's compartment, causing multiple lacerations to Dmitryi's legs and rendering him unconscious. The smoldering BMP was dead in its tracks. They were sitting ducks, only partially hidden under the flimsy bridge.

Colonel Boruff overflew the bridge to the south, then rapidly slowed and turned the craft to the north. Flying above the dirt road toward the BMP, the gunner opened fire with the chin gun, spraying the area under the bridge with the heavy caliber rounds. The electric turret of the Dagger was still operational, and Tariq swung the cannon around and opened fire on the Hind. Several tracer rounds zipped toward the helicopter, striking the empty gun pod and just missing the cockpit.

Boruff immediately realized that the predator had become the prey and desperately maneuvered his craft out of the line of fire. He pushed the throttles forward while hauling back on the collective, floating the big craft up and over the bridge, turning 180 degrees as he did. He planned to drop down on the north side of the bridge behind the Dagger to finish the fight away from the vehicle's cannon.

Pete spotted the helicopter through his vision block and screamed aloud to the crew. "THE DOG HAS COME AROUND TO THE NORTH SIDE! HE IS ABOUT TO ATT—" His words were cut short as a hail of bullets from the Hind's chin gun fell upon the Dagger. The helicopter had settled into attack position just thirty feet off the deck and fifty yards away. After several bursts, the Russian gunner reported that the gun had jammed, and Boruff ordered him to open fire with the remaining rocket pod. The colonel knew that at such short range, the attack would be devastating.

The sixteen rockets ripped into the Dagger, igniting most of the reactive armor covering the vehicle. The exploding armor worked as advertised, diverting the explosions outward, though the vehicle was virtually destroyed by the attack. Graze shook his head to clear the ringing and willed himself to remain conscious. The intercom was dead, and for all he knew, the entire crew was also dead. He popped open his hatch and climbed out of the burning wreckage, choking on the heavy smoke. He knew he had just seconds to find the one remaining weapon that could be used to take down the enemy helicopter. Scrambling to the rear of the vehicle, he opened the troop door, screaming, "STINGER! I NEED THE STINGER!" From within the smoke-filled compartment, a pair of bloodied hands reached out with the weapon he sought.

Meanwhile, the Hind crew were congratulating themselves with excitement as the thick blue-gray clouds of smoke poured out from under the bridge. The colonel backed away and rose to an altitude of 200 feet to avoid any damage from secondary explosions. Boruff congratulated his gunner. "Good work. We killed the rats. Time to report in. I'll request ground support to pick up the bodies."

The colonel looked down at his instrument panel to change radio frequencies but was interrupted by the shout of his Gunner. "What in the world? It isn't possible! Colonel, Look!" Both men were shocked at what they saw emerging from the thick smoke billowing out from under the bridge. Walking towards them was a solitary man, but not just any man. A tall American in blue jeans, pointy-toed boots, and a ball cap was looking right at them and holding up the middle finger of his left hand. Too late, they realized that his right hand held a missile launcher being rapidly raised to his shoulder.

The colonel slammed the throttles and cranked back on the collective, urging the helicopter up and away, desperately trying to escape. The helicopter slowly began to turn and climb as both airmen's eyes locked on the figure below them. The gunner's fingers had just reached the chaff/flare dispenser switch when a puff of smoke announced the Stinger's short flight had begun. The heat-seeking warhead had readily locked onto the massive thermal signature of the starboard engine. Two seconds later, the missile tore through the engine and exploded in the transmission below the massive rotors.

The spinning five-bladed rotor immediately began to disintegrate, flying away with centrifugal energy in every direction. One blade came off the helicopter nearly intact and spun out across the wheat field like a giant boomerang. The blade was still flying away as the helicopter stalled and seemed to stop in mid-air, floating in slow motion just a few hundred feet away. Graze ducked reflexively as the craft fell straight down, landing with a ground-shaking thump, followed by a fireballl.

Dropping the spent launcher, Graze immediately turned his attention to the crew. The smoke had started to clear, and he was amazed to see four of the men evacuating the smoldering Dagger. He climbed onto the front of the vehicle and pried open the driver's hatch to find Dmytryi still barely alive. Spotting Pavel, Graze yelled, "Pavel, help me with Dmytryi!" The two pulled him free and carried him away from the burning wreckage. The other three limped or crawled up onto the roadway fearing the BMP would explode at any second.

They gathered in stunned silence for a few minutes, overwhelmed by the miracle of their escape. Pavel was the first to speak, looking towards the burning Hind. "Graze, was it you that got him with the Stinger? I just remember the hatch opening and someone grabbing the missile from my hands."

"Yes, thank God you had it ready. I doubt I could have found it otherwise."

All of the men were covered in grime, soot, and blood, though none of the injuries seemed immediately life-threatening. Dmytryi had lost a lot of blood from the deep lacerations to both legs, but tourniquets had stemmed the flow. He was moaning in pain as he regained consciousness, lying with his head in Pete's lap. Pete himself was soaked in blood, despite the tourniquet. Pavel and Aleksandr seemed to be the least injured, so they returned to the Dagger to retrieve the medical kit, water, and small arms for the group.

After Graze extinguished the last of the fires in the

vehicle, he searched his compartment and the turret for any usable communication equipment but found little that was useful or undamaged. When he noticed three holes in the chair back, he frantically checked himself for injuries, but his kevlar vest had spared him. He was surprised that he was not killed in the small compartment. There were several jagged holes in the metal, and the electronic equipment was shot to pieces.

The six men gathered on the road in a rag-tag group, tending to their wounds and drinking water. Pavel had brought some rations from the troop compartment, but none of the crew had an appetite—in fact, they were all still in a state of shock from the battle. After a few minutes, Graze took a long drink of water and cleared his throat, "Men, the Dagger is finished, and we are still at least 35 klicks from the Ukrainian lines. It won't be long until the Russians are upon us. We can't run or hide, and we won't be able to defend ourselves for long when they find us."

"True," said Pete. "Surely the helicopters or the soldiers at the checkpoint have reported our position."

"And if not," Pavel added, " they can easily follow the trail of burning equipment and dead Russians we left behind."

Aleksandr raised his water bottle in a toast, "Here's to dead Russians!"

Pete had placed a rolled-up tunic under Dmytryi's head,

and he stood to address the men. "It's true that we did our mission better than anyone could have imagined, but we have arrived at the end game now, and our escape from here is not likely. When they find us, we will give them hell, but you all understand that capture is not an option. We know too much, and we are wearing Russian uniforms. I don't intend to be tortured to death by those bast—"

A deafening boom overhead cut short the general's words, causing everyone to reflexively hit the ground. All of the men quickly recognized the sound of low-flying jets passing directly overhead. "Hey!" yelled Pavel, "those are *Ukrainian* MIGs, not Russian!" The jets were flying at treetop level and maximum speed, all heavily laden with bombs on their wings. As soon as the aircraft disappeared to the east, another group of at least 25 slower SU-24 and SU-25 attack aircraft flew overhead with the same deafening roar. The crew watched as ten of the craft peeled off, heading southeast towards Crimea. With the Russian Air Defense network down, Operation Sunflower was now in full motion.

"YES!!" Graze said excitedly as he realized what was happening. "We opened the door for the Air Force by taking out the Air Defense Command Center. Now it's up to them to finish the job."

"Absolutely true," Pete added, "but it's not only the Air Force. Right now, we are throwing everything we have at them on land and sea also. This will be the start of a great

Ukrainian victory, men."

"That is great news, General," replied Pavel, "but I prefer to celebrate with my family if possible. Do we have any chance to get out of here?"

Graze answered, "Colonel Stapleton promised to be waiting for us on the Ukrainian lines. If there was some way we could signal to him, we might yet get out of here alive."

"Right," Alex replied. "No cell phones, no radios. What's left? Smoke signals?"

Just then, Graze noticed an item in the small pile of items scavenged from the Dagger. "Wait a minute, what about this?" He picked up the infrared strobe they had used earlier that morning and switched it on. The unit was undamaged and seemed to be still operational. The men were optimistic that the strobe could be used to contact the Ukrainians, but Graze quickly pointed out that it could not be seen at such a great distance even if someone were looking for them. It seemed there was nothing more to do.

A pall of hopeless resignation seemed to fall upon the men as they quietly settled on the roadway. As the wind picked up speed, they all could see the dark clouds of a storm front approaching from the south. Pete was going around to each of the men passing out water, food, and ammunition while trying to lift their spirits. He paused, looking south at the approaching storm and said to no one in particular, "The rain has been our friend more than once these past few days.

Maybe the rain will hide us again." Noting the wind, Aleksandr remarked sarcastically that it was good weather for kites, at least.

After a short pause, Tariq jumped to his feet and shouted to Graze, "That's it! A kite! What if we flew the strobe higher? Could they see it then?"

Graze instantly grasped the potential of the idea and grabbed his old friend by the shoulders, answering with excitement, "Yes, if we could get the strobe up a couple hundred feet, it might just work, but do we have what we need?"

"I don't know, Graze. We need a frame, some fabric, a line, and a tail."

Pavel jumped in then. "We can use aluminum parts from the seats in the Dagger for the frame and Pete's flag. We have shirts for a tail."

"Great!" answered Tariq, "but what about the line?" Aleksandr reminded them that there was duct tape and several hundred meters of thin wire for the guided missile stored in the vehicle.

Suddenly, the crew was energized by the hope of escape and gathered the materials from the Dagger for Tariq to build the most important kite he would ever make. Graze began re-programming the strobe while the other men worked on the make-shift kite. T-shirts were torn into strips for the tail, and the strobe was taped to the frame. The tape was also used to patch several holes in the tattered Ukrainian flag. In less than fifteen minutes, Tariq declared they were ready to try it. While Pavel walked the rickety kite downwind, Pete whispered to Graze, "I hope he knows what he is doing because that is one ugly kite."

"Cross your fingers, General."

The first two attempts to get the kite airborne failed, with Tariq adjusting the kite and the tail after each try. On the third try, Pavel walked the kite two hundred feet downwind and waited for Tariq's signal. Graze stood next to his old friend and said, "You got this, buddy. Everyone knows that the third time is—"

"—is the charms, baby!" Tariq finished the sentence signaling Pavel to let go.

The jury-rigged flag finally took flight, as the Kite Runner of Kabul plied his skill. The men erupted in cheers and applause, watching the kite soar in the sky above them. Graze silently mouthed a prayer, asking for divine intervention, "Please, God, let Colonel Stapleton see this signal."

The wind was steadily picking up speed, making the kite harder to control. Tariq tugged and wrestled with the heavy kite for several minutes, eventually calling for Alex to help hold the line. Three times it dove towards the ground, eliciting gasps from the men, but Tariq regained control, accompanied by the cheers and shouts of everyone.

Graze checked his watch and noted that their signal had been flying for seven minutes. "You are doing great, man!" he called out to Tariq. "Keep it up as long as you can!"

Pete, still standing with Graze, quietly asked, "You *did* turn the strobe on, right?"

Graze's eyes grew wide, and he gave the general a shocked look, then smiled and winked an affirmative.

Thirty seconds later, a strong gust of wind snapped the frame, and the horrified men watched as the kite fluttered and flapped slowly to the ground, crashing hard on the roadway. Pavel ran to retrieve it but was dejected to find that the frame was destroyed, the flag torn, and the strobe smashed to pieces. They had played their last card and had no idea if their signal had been seen or if anyone was even looking for them.

True to his word, Colonel Mark Stapleton was definitely looking for them. In fact, he was just 35 klicks from their position in the right seat of a Ukrainian MI-8 helicopter hovering at 1,000 feet just behind the Ukrainian lines. There were four medics with stretchers and first aid supplies in the back of the craft. Together with the pilot, Mark was anxiously scanning the horizon and monitoring the radios for any sign of the Dagger. Suddenly the pilot clicked on the intercom and reported, "Colonel, our infrared sensors are picking up a faint signal to our southeast. It appears to be pulsing in morse code."

Mark donned his infrared goggles and scanned to the southeast. He could just make out the signal and began to write on a pad the dots and dashes as best he could tell: --. / .-./ .- / -... / . Underneath the code, he wrote the letters G R A B E. Grabe? He checked the flashing code again and spoke the letters aloud. "G . . . R . . . A . . . wait!" The fourth letter was a Z, not a B. "GRAZE!" he shouted. "It's him; it's the Dagger!" Then to the pilot, "Get us on the deck at max speed towards that signal." The pilot immediately pushed the throttles forward and headed southeast at two hundred feet. A minute later, the signal quit, and the pilot did his best to maintain his heading, though the high winds were complicating their course.

They had traveled about 25 km when Mark spotted a column of black smoke and ordered the pilot towards it. They soon arrived at the crash site of the first Hind, burning beside an east-west blacktop road. Mark put two and two together and calculated that if, in fact, the Dagger had downed the Russian chopper, they had most likely proceeded west on the road, so he ordered the pilot to head in that direction. Both men quickly spotted another smoke column in a field just north of a small bridge. As the helicopter slowed to inspect the wreckage, the pilot noticed a group of men huddled on the roadway. "Colonel, look by the bridge! Is that the crew?"

"Oh my god, it has to be them. Quick! Show them who we are!"

The crew of the Dagger was now helplessly gathered on the roadway, tending the wounded among them and drinking the last of their water. The first sprinkles of refreshing rain had begun to fall on the exhausted crew as the dark clouds rolled towards them across the fields. They sat with their heads tilted up, letting the gentle rain wash their bloodied faces. The cool breeze felt so good; the men relished the small comfort and perhaps forgot for a moment just how hopeless their situation was.

Tariq heard it first and stood up, facing east. "LISTEN! DO YOU HEAR IT?" Within moments they all heard the sound of a helicopter approaching from the east. Pistol Pete stood up shakily and spoke to the crew. "This is it, men. The Russians have found us. We will go down fighting and die with honor. Get your weapons ready. Wait until I open fire, then give the dogs everything you have." The men knew that they had zero hope of defeating the heavy weapons on the helicopter but prepared with grim determination.

Graze checked the mag on his 9 mm pistol and stood next to his dear friend, Tariq, with his arm around his shoulder. "You are the best friend I ever had, Tariq. You saved my life more than once, but I'm afraid I can't return the favor today. Are you ready?"

Tariq looked his friend in the eyes and confidently stated,

"Allahu Akbar."

Graze smiled. "Yes, God is great."

The entire group briefly hugged or shook hands, making the best of this short goodbye. The sign of the cross was repeated by all, even Tariq, in solidarity with his friends. Dmytryi, now conscious, was propped against the guard rail with an AK-74 in his hands. Pete stepped towards the approaching craft, cocked, and raised his Colt 45, "Get ready to fire on my command!"

As they watched the helicopter slowly approach, the enemy craft did a very odd thing. The helicopter turned its side towards them and continued to hover slowly closer. In that position, the rocket and gun pods were not trained on their position, and the helicopter was most vulnerable to fire. Pete was about to squeeze the trigger when he saw the Ukrainian flag on the fuselage and yelled, "Hold your fire; it's Ukrainian!"

The men shouted with joy and waved as the big bulbous helicopter landed on the roadway thirty yards from them. Mark Stapleton was the first one out the door, followed by the medics with stretchers and medical supplies. While the medics loaded Dmytryi on a stretcher, the other men gathered around Mark amid the roar of the engines and the downwash. Pete joked in a loud voice to Mark, "You are lucky I didn't blast you with my Colt!"

"Who are you kidding?" Mark shouted in response,

"You couldn't hit a barn with that peashooter!" The rain was gaining intensity, and the pilot asked permission to take off. Mark told the pilot to wait another minute, then handed the headset to Pete and shouted to him again, "Get everyone on board and ready for takeoff. I'll be right behind you. There is one last thing to do."

The Dagger had performed beyond anyone's expectations, and perhaps one day, the history books would tell the incredible story of its role in Operation Sunflower. Though the vehicle was virtually destroyed, many of the sophisticated western systems were inside, and it could not be allowed to fall into Russian hands.

Mark grabbed an incendiary grenade and ducked under the bridge just far enough to lob it into the pool of fuel under the smoldering machine. He was nearly back to the waiting helicopter when the vehicle exploded and began to burn. Pete was waiting in the doorway and pointed down the road where Pavel was retrieving the broken flag kite.

"Actually," shouted Pete with a smile, "there are *two* last things."

Epilogue

It was a beautiful, warm September day in upstate New York. Jerry had been sailing for nearly three hours up and down the pristine lake. The wind had settled down to about 7 knots, and he was smoothly gliding down wind, on a broad reach, towards his dock. In fact, Jerry sailed every chance he could since returning to his home on June 15. He scanned the lake, set the wheel lock to hold his heading, and retrieved his phone and an ice-cold Genny Cream from below decks. Jan and her family and other local friends would be arriving soon for lunch at the cottage, and Jerry reminded himself to light the grill as soon as he docked in about twenty minutes.

He checked the lake for traffic once more and stretched out in the cockpit, relishing the warm September sun while turning over the events of the past four months. The Ukrainian counteroffensive that began on May 25, 2022, lasted three days. The Dagger mission had disabled Russian air defenses and killed three-fourths of the senior Russian staff at a breakfast party in Eastern Ukraine. On day two, Russian forces launched a half-hearted counterattack against the Ukrainian base at Dnipro, but the Trap Door defenses and Ukrainian air force turned their route into the Highway of Death. By the morning of May 27, Russian soldiers were deserting *en masse* and beginning the long walk back to mother Russia.

The stunning defeat of the Russian army shocked the entire world, though everyone feared that Putin's reaction might include nuclear weapons. On the morning of day three at 0900, the red telephone—the hotline to Moscow—rang on President Joe Biden's desk, but Putin was not calling. Dmitry Medvedev, Deputy Chairman of the Security Council, and a dozen other generals and leaders of the Russian government were on the line instead. Vladimir Putin, they explained, had fled the country on the day before, possibly to Iran, though they could not be certain.

Medvelev was acting president and wished to convey four important points:

1. The war was over.

2. Russia's nuclear arsenal was under his control, and there would be no nuclear response.

3. An immediate cease-fire order had been issued to all Russian military units.

4. Russian forces would withdraw from all Ukrainian territory to be replaced by UN peacekeeping forces as soon as possible.

The military aid flowing into Ukraine soon shifted to food, fuel, and construction materials as hundreds of thousands of displaced Ukrainians returned home to pick up the pieces of their broken lives and homes. Tariq and his family emigrated to the U.S. in July of 2022, joining the large community of Afghani immigrants that had settled in Lincoln, Nebraska. He had called Jerry a few days prior with news of a full-time job at the Kawasaki Rail Car factory in Lincoln.

The events that began for Jerry with a late-night phone call four months ago seemed almost surreal now. It felt like a lifetime ago and yesterday simultaneously. He laughed to himself when thinking of Pistol Pete with his grand mustache and pearl-handled Colt. Jerry's smile turned into something else when he remembered the bravery and sacrifice of the Wolverines, however.

Yes, Jerry was in a good place now, personally, but his happiness was bittersweet, plagued as he was by two very big unresolved matters that were always at the front of his mind. Ailana was the first of them. He had not spoken with her since the night he left Poland with the crew of the Dagger. She hadn't returned any of his calls or texts, yet he could not stop thinking about her. The second matter was the escape of Putin following the defeat of his army. Putin was the subject of the largest manhunt in human history, and Jerry could not help but think his mission was not complete until the butcher was brought to justice.

Jerry was now three hundred yards from the dock and focused on the business of sailing. He furled the jib and turned into the wind, setting the craft in irons in order to lower the main. Waving to Jan and his nephews waiting on the dock, he noted that his other guests had also begun arriving. He watched his contractor friends park and start for the cottage — no doubt with their buddy Captain Morgan in Kelly's cooler.

Jerry had just dropped the main sail when the satellite phone began to ring for the first time since returning home. There was only one person who had the number—Colonel Mark Stapleton. The call only lasted a few minutes, leaving Jerry with a huge grin as he hung up. He might not be able to fix his Ailana problem, but it sounded like he was going to get a chance to help solve the Putin problem.

Jan and her boys watched as Jerry lowered the sails, fired up the diesel, and gracefully maneuvered towards the dock and his waiting guests. The youngest nephew, Matthew, turned towards his mom. "Did Uncle Jerry get a new boat?"

Eyeing the freshly painted words on the transom, Jan replied, "No honey, he just changed the name. Now get ready to toss your uncle the dock line."

Matthew watched as the sailboat slowly glided toward him and wondered to himself, "Where did he come up with *The Kite?*"

www.ingramcontent.com/pod-product-compliance
Lightning Source LLC
Chambersburg PA
CBHW070635170726
48291CB00003B/1022